# Vergilius

## A Tale of the Coming of Christ

By

### Irving Bacheller

Author of
" Eben Holden " " D'ri and I "
" Darrel of the Blessed Isles "

New York and London
Harper & Brothers Publishers
1904

# Vergilius

## A Tale of the Coming of Christ

# Chapter

## 1

ROME had passed the summits and stood looking into the dark valley of fourteen hundred years. Behind her the graves of Cæsar and Sallust and Cicero and Catullus and Vergil and Horace; before her centuries of madness and treading down; round about her a multitude sickening of luxury, their houses filled with spoil, their mouths with folly, their souls with discontent; above her only mystery and silence; in her train, philosophers questioning if it were not better for a man had he never been born—deeming life a misfortune and ex-

3

tinction the only happiness; poets singing
no more of "pleasantries and trifles," but
seeking favor with poor obscenities. Soon
they were even to celebrate the virtue of
harlots, the integrity of thieves, the tender-
ness of murderers, the justice of oppression.
Leading the caravan were types abhorrent
and self-opposed—effeminate men, mascu-
line women, cheerful cynics, infidel priests,
wealthy people with no credit, patricians,
honoring and yet despising the gods, hating
and yet living on the populace. Here was
the spectacle of a republican empire, and an
emperor gathering power while he affected
to disdain it.

The splendor of the capital had attracted
from all nations the idle rich, gamblers,
speculators, voluptuaries, profligates, in-
triguers, criminals. To such an extreme
had luxury been carried that nothing was
too sacred, nothing too costly to be enjoyed.
Digestion had become a science, courtship
an art, sleep a nightmare, comfort an ac-
complishment, and the very act of living an

4

industry. Almost one may say that the gods lived only in the imagination of the ignorant and the jests of the learned. In a growing patriciate home had become a weariness, marriage a form, children a trouble, and the decline of motherhood an alarming fact. Augustus tried the remedy of legislation. Henceforth marriage became a duty to the state. As between men and women, things were near a turning-point. Woman cannot long endure scorn nor the absence of veneration. A law older than the tablets of stone shall be her defence. Love is the price of motherhood. Soon or late, unless it be mingled in some degree with her passion, the wonderful gift is withdrawn and men cease to be born of her. Slowly, both the bitterness and the understanding of its loss turn the world to virtue. A new and lofty sentiment was appearing. Woman, weary of her part in the human comedy, had begun to inspire a love sublime as the miracle in which she is born to act.

5

Happily, there were good people in Rome, even noble families, with whom sacrifice had still a sacred power, and who practised the four virtues of honor, bravery, wisdom, and temperance. In rural Latium, rich and poor clung to the old faith, and everywhere a plebeian feared alike the assessor and the gods, and sacrificed to both.

It is no wonder the gods were falling when even Jupiter had been outdone by a modest man who dwelt on the Palatine. One might have seen him there any day— a rather delicate figure with shiny blue eyes and hair now turning gray. He flung his lightning with unerring aim across the great purple sea into Arabia, Africa, and Spain, and northward to the German Ocean and eastward to the land of the Goths. The genius of this remarkable man had outdone the imagination of priest and poet. A genius for organization, like that of his illustrious uncle, gave to Augustus a power greater than human hands had yet wielded.

6

A bit of gossip had travelled far and excited his curiosity. It spoke of a new king, with power above that of men, who was to conquer the world. Sayings of certain learned men came out of Judea into the land of lost hope. They told of the king of promise—that he would bring to men the gift of immortal life, that the heavens would declare his authority. Superstitious to the blood and bone, not a few were thrilled by the message.

The minds of thinking men were sad, fearful, and beset with curiosity. "If there be no gods," they were wont to ask, "have we any hope and responsibility?" They studied the philosophers Plato, Aristotle, Zeno, Epicurus, and were unsatisfied.

The nations were at peace, but not the souls of men. A universal and mighty war of the spirit was near at hand. The skirmishers were busy—patrician and plebeian, master and slave, oppressor and oppressed. Soon all were to see the line of battle, the immortal captains, the children of darkness,

7

the children of light, the beginning of a great revolution.

Rome was like a weary child whose toys are gods and men, and who, being weary of them, has yet a curiosity in their destruction.

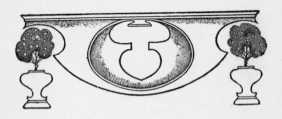

## Chapter 2

HOSE days it was near twelve o'clock by the great dial of history. One day, about mid-afternoon, the old capital lay glowing in the sunlight. Its hills were white with marble and green with gardens, and traced and spotted and flecked with gold; its thoroughfares were bright with color—white, purple, yellow, scarlet—like a field of roses and amarantus.

The fashionable day had begun; knight and lady were now making and receiving visits.

Five litters and some forty slaves, who

bore and followed them, were waiting in
the court of the palace of the Lady Lucia.
Beyond the walls of white marble a noble
company was gathered that summer day.
There were the hostess and her daughter;
three young noblemen, the purple stripes
on each angusticlave telling of knightly
rank; a Jewish prince in purple and gold;
an old philosopher, and a poet who had
been reading love lines. It was the age
of pagan chivalry, and one might imperil
his future with poor wit or a faulty epi-
gram. Those older men had long held the
floor, and their hostess, seeking to rally the
young knights, challenged their skill in
courtly compliment.

"O men, who have forgotten the love of
women these days, look at her!"

So spoke the Lady Lucia—she that was
widow of the Præfect Publius, who fell
with half his cohort in the desert wars.

She had risen from a chair of ebony enriched by cunning Etruscan art — four
mounted knights charging across its heavy

back in armor of wrought gold. She stopped, facing the company, between two columns of white marble beautifully sculptured. Upon each a vine rose, limberly and with soft leaves in the stone, from base to capital. Her daughter stood in the midst of a group of maids who were dressing her hair.

"Arria, will you come to me?" said the Lady Lucia.

The girl came quickly—a dainty creature of sixteen, her dark hair waving, under jewelled fillets, to a knot behind. From below the knot a row of curls fell upon the folds of her outer tunic. It was a filmy, transparent thing—this garment—through which one could see the white of arm and breast and the purple fillets on her legs.

"She is indeed beautiful in the yellow tunic. I should think that scarlet rug had caught fire and wrapped her in its flame," said the poet Ovid.

"Nay, her heart is afire, and its light hath the color of roses," said an old phi-

11

losopher who sat by. "Can you not see it shining through her cheeks?"

"Young sirs," said the Lady Lucia, with a happy smile, as she raised her daughter's hand, "now for your offers."

It was a merry challenge, and shows how lightly they treated a sacred theme those days.

First rose the grave senator, Aulus Valerius Maro by name.

"Madame," said he, stepping forward and bowing low, "I offer my heart and my fortune, and the strength of my arms and the fleetness of my feet and the fair renown of my fathers."

The Lady Lucia turned to her daughter with a look of inquiry.

"Brave words are not enough," said the fair Roman maiden, smiling, as her eyes fell.

Then came the effeminate Gracus, in head-dress and neckerchief, frilled robe and lady's sandals. He was of great sires who had borne the Roman eagles into Gaul.

"Good lady," said he, "I would give my life."

"And had I more provocation," said Arria, raising a jewelled bodkin, "I would take it."

Now the splendid Antipater, son of Herod the Great, was up and speaking. "I offer," said he, "my heart and wealth and half my hopes, and the jewels of my mother, and a palace in the beautiful city of Jerusalem."

"And a pretty funeral," the girl remarked, thoughtfully. "Jerusalem is half-way to Hades."

The Roman matron turned, and put her arm around the waist of the girl and drew her close. A young man rose from his chair and approached them. He was Vergilius, son of Varro, and of equestrian knighthood. His full name was Quintus Vergilius Varro, but all knew the youth by his nomen. Tall and erect, with curly, blond locks and blue eyes and lips delicately curved, there was in that hall no

13

ancestral mask or statue so nobly favored.
He had been taught by an old philosopher
to value truth as the better part of honor—
a view not common then, but therein was
a new light, spreading mysteriously.

"Dear Lady Lucia," said he, "I cannot
amuse you with idle words. I fear to
speak, and yet silence would serve me ill.
I offer not the strength of my arms nor the
fleetness of my feet, for they may fail me to-
morrow; nor my courage, for that has never
been tried; nor the renown of my fathers,
for that is not mine to give; nor my life, for
that belongs to my country; nor my fortune,
for I should blush to offer what may be used
to buy cattle. I would give a thing greater
and more lasting than all of these. It is
my love."

The girl turned half away, blushing pink.
All had flung off the mask of comedy and
now wore a look of surprise.

"By my faith!" said the poet, "this
young knight meant his words."

"A man of sincerity, upon my soul!" said

the old philosopher. "I have put my hope in him, and so shall Rome. A lucky girl is she, for has he not riches, talent, honor, temperance, courage, and the beauty of a god? And was I not his teacher?"

"My brave Vergilius," the matron answered, "you are like the knights of old I have heard my father tell of. They had such a way with them—never a smile and a melancholy look in their faces when they spoke of love. I give you the crown of gallantry, and, if she be willing, you shall walk with her in the garden. That is your reward."

Vergilius, advancing, took the girl's hand and kissed it.

"Will you go with me?" said he.

"On one condition," she answered, looking down at the folds of her tunic.

"And it is?"

"That you will entertain me with philosophy and the poets," she answered, with a smile.

"And with no talk of love," the matron added, as Arria took his arm.

They walked through the long hall of the palace, over soft rugs and great mosaics, and between walls aglow with tints of sky and garden. These two bore with them a tender feeling as they passed the figures of embattled horse and host in carven wood, and mural painting and colored mosaic and wrought metal — symbols of the martial spirit of the empire now oddly in contrast with their own. They came out upon a peristyle overlooking an ample garden wherein were vines, flowers, and fruit trees.

"You have a way of words," said she. "It is almost possible to believe you."

He stopped and for a long moment looked into her eyes. "I love you, sweet girl," he said, softly; "I love you. As I live, I speak the truth."

"And you a man!" she exclaimed, incredulously.

"Ay, strange as it may be, a Roman."

"My mother has told me," said she, looking down at her sandal, "that when a

16

man speaks, it is well to listen but never to believe."

"They are not easy to understand—these men and women," said he, thoughtfully. "Sometimes I think they would be nobler if they were dumb as dogs. Albeit I suppose they would find a new way of lying. But, O sweet sister of Appius, try to believe me, though you believe no other, and I—I shall believe you always."

"You had better not," said she, with a merry glance.

"I must."

"But you will doubt me soon, for I shall say that I do not love you."

For a little he knew not how to answer. She turned away, looking off at the Capitoline, where the toil and art of earth had wrought to show the splendor of heaven. Its beautiful, barbaric temples were glowing in the sunlight.

"Life would be too serious if there were no dissimulation." She looked up at him

17

as she spoke, and he saw a little quiver in her curved lips.

"That bow of your lips—I should think it fashioned by Praxiteles—and it is for the arrows of truth."

"But a girl—she must deceive a little."

They were now among the vines.

"I do not understand you."

"Stupid fellow!" said she, in a whisper, as she turned, looking up at him. "Son of Varo, lovers are not ever to be trusted. Shall I tell you a story? One day I was in the Via Sacra and a young man caught and held me for a moment and tried to touch my lips—that boy, Antipater, a good-looking wretch!"

She gave her shoulders a little shrug and drew her robe closer. "He had come out of the Basilica Julia, and I am sure he had been over-drinking. I cried 'Help!' and quickly a man came and stood between us; and oh! young sir, as I live, it was our great father Augustus, and Antipater knelt before him.

18

"'Young man,' said the father — and his eyes shone — 'rise and look yonder. Do you see the citadel? Under its marble floor there is a grave. It is that of one who kissed a vestal and was buried alive. There are sacred people in Rome, and among them is this daughter of my beloved Publius. Go you to your palace, son of Herod, and, hereafter, forget not that you are in Rome.'

"He was angry, and I, so frightened! Then he took me home and said he would be my father, and that in good time he would choose a husband for me."

"The gods grant that he choose me."

"The gods forbid it, son of Varro."

"And why?"

Slowly and with assumed severity she spoke. "Because — I — do — not — love — you."

"Cruel one!" said he, turning and biting his lips. "Your words are as the blow of the pilum."

"Have they indeed wounded you?" She touched his hand with a look of sympathy.

19

"They have made me sick at heart."

"Then would I not believe them," said she, tenderly, slipping her slender fingers into his.

He pressed her hand. "And do you, then, love me?"

"No—I—do—not—love—you."

"You are a strange people—you maidens of the capital," said he, taking her hand in both of his. "Rome has conquered everything save its women."

She parted her tunic and stood looking down at her white bosom, and with her delicate fingers brushed off a bit of dust which had fallen from the vine above them.

"I do think much of love," said she, thoughtfully, still looking down at her breast.

"And of me," he insisted.

"Nay, not of you," she answered, without delay.

"I shall know," said he, wistfully, "for I shall consult the fates. I have here a sacred coin. An old dame found it when

20

she was digging in the side of Soracte.
See, it has on its face the head of Apollo,
and opposite is an arrow in a death-
hand. And the hag had an odd dream
of this coin, so she told me — that it fell
out of the sky, and was, indeed, from the
treasury of the gods, and had in it a wonderful power in all mysteries. And one
might tell by tossing it in the air and noting
its fall, if he were loved or hated by the
first one he should see after learning its
answer. I have never known it to fail.
If the head is up you love me," said he,
tossing the disk of metal.

It fell and lay at his feet.

"The head!" he exclaimed, with joy.

"Is it really blest of the gods?" she inquired, eagerly, her cheeks aflame. "Is it
indeed blest?"

"So said the woman who gave it me."

"Now I shall toss it," said she, taking the
coin.

"Ah! you would know if I love you," he
answered.

The coin leaped high and fell and rolled along the marble walk. Both followed eagerly, he leading, and, as it stopped, he quickly covered the bit of metal with his hand.

"Let me see!" said she, her hand upon his wrist.

"Do not look."

"Let me see it!" she insisted.

"Sweet sister of Appius, I beg of you, here on my knees, do not look at the coin! I will give you the white steeds from Cappadocia, but do not look."

"Let me see it, I say, son of Varro!" She was tugging at his wrist, and now, indeed, there was a pretty pleading in her voice. The words were to him as pearls strung on a silken thread.

"Wait a little."

"I shall not wait."

"Sweet flower of Rome," said he, looking into her eyes, "I know that you are mine now! Your voice—it is like the love-call of the robin!"

22

"Stubborn boy! Do you think I care for you?" She stopped and looked into his eyes.

"Else why should you wish to see the coin?" said he. "But, look! Upon my soul it is false!" A little silence followed.

"'Tis false!" he repeated. "I swear the coin lies, for I do love you, dearly."

"It does not lie," she whispered.

He put his arm about her.

"And I know," he answered, "why you think it cannot lie. It said, before, that you love me, and it was right."

She thrust him away gently, and, rising, as if stricken with sudden fear of him, ran a few paces up the walk. She turned quickly, and looked back at him as he approached. Her face had grown pale.

"I—I shall never speak with you again," she whispered.

"Oh, have mercy upon me, beautiful sister of Appius!" said the young knight, and there was a note of despair in his voice. "Have mercy upon me!"

"Young sir," said she, retreating slowly, as he advanced, "I do not love you—I do not love you."

She turned quickly, and ran to the peristyle, and, stopping not to glance back at him, entered the great marble home of her fathers.

He stood a moment looking at the sunglow behind roof and dome and tower. A bridge of light, spanning the hollow of the city, had laid its golden timbers from hill to hill; and for a little the young man felt as if he were drowning in the shadows under it. He turned presently and hurried into the palace.

## Chapter

### 3

"HE is more honored than Jupiter these days," the philosopher was saying as Vergilius re-entered.

"Who?" inquired the young man.

"Who else but Cæsar, and it is well. The gods—who are they?"

"The adopted children of Vergil and Homer," said Appius, brother of Arria, who had just returned from the baths.

"But our great father Augustus—who can doubt that he deserves our worship?" said the philosopher, a subtle irony in his voice. It was this learned man who had long been the instructor of Vergilius.

"Who, indeed?" was the remark of another.

"But these gods!"

"At least they are not likely to cut off one's head," said Aulus.

"Speak not lightly of the gods," said Vergilius. "They are still a power with the people, and the people have great need of them. What shall become of Rome when the gods fall?"

"It shall sicken," said the philosopher, with a lift of his hand. "You that are young may live to see the end. It shall be like the opening of the underworld. Our republic is false, our gods are false, and, indeed, I know but one truth."

"And what may it be?" said another.

"We are all liars," he quickly answered.

"O tempora!" said the Lady Lucia. "It is an evil day, especially among men. When Quinta Claudia went with her noble sisters to meet the Idæan mother at Terracina they were able to find in Rome one virtuous man to escort them. But

26

that was more than two hundred years ago."

"If one were to find him now, and he were to go," said the philosopher, "by the gods above us! I fear he would return a sad rake indeed."

"'Tis not a pleasant theme," said the Lady Lucia, by way of introducing another.

"The dear old girl!" said young Gracus, in a low tone, as he turned to the senator. "Her hair is a lie, her complexion is a lie, her lips are a lie."

"And her life is a lie," said the other.

"You enjoyed your walk?" asked the mother of Arria, addressing Vergilius.

"The walk was a delight to me and its end a sorrow," he answered.

"And you obeyed me?"

"To the letter." It is true, he thought, we are a generation of liars, but how may one help it? Then, quickly, a way seemed to suggest itself, and he added: "Madame, forgive me. I do now remember we had a word or two about love; but, you see, I was

27

telling the legend of this coin. It has the power to show one if he be loved."

"By tossing?"

"By tossing. Head, yes; the reverse, no."

"Let me try." She flung it to the oaken beams and it fell on the great rug beside her.

"Madame, the hand is up," said Vergilius. "I fear it is not infallible."

"Let me see," she answered, stooping gravely to survey the coin. Something passed between her and her pleasure, and for one second a shadow wavered across her face.

"It is Death's hand, of course," she remarked, sadly. "Love is for the young and death is for the old."

"Old, madame! Why, your cheeks have roses in them."

"Good youth, you are too frank," said she, with a quick glance about her. "Did the coin say that she loved you?"

"It did."

28

And what did she say?"

The young man hesitated.

"Come, you innocent! Of course, I knew that you would talk of nothing but love. What said she?"

"That she does not love me; but I am sure it is mere coquetry."

"Dear youth! You have a cunning eye. This very day speak, my brave Vergilius— speak to her brother Appius. To - night take him to dine with you."

"I had so planned."

A gong of silver rang in the palace halls. It was the signal to prepare for dinner, and the guests made their farewells. Soon Appius and the young lover walked side by side in the direction of the Palatine.

"And what have you been doing?" the former inquired, presently.

"Only dreaming."

"Of what?"

"Of love and happiness, and your sister."

"My sister?"

29

"Yes; I love her and wish to make her my wife."

"You have wealth and birth and wit and good prospects. I can see no objection to you. But love—love is a thing for women to talk about."

"You are wrong, Appius. I can feel it in my soul. And, believe me, I am no longer in Rome. I have found the gateway of a better world—like that heaven they speak of in the Trastevere—full of peace and beauty."

"You have, indeed, been dreaming," said the other. "But, Vergilius, there is one higher than I who shall choose her husband—the imperator. Does he know you?"

"I have met him, of course, but do much fear he would not remember me."

"We may know shortly. Every seventh day this year he has sat, like a beggar, at his gate asking for alms. To-day we shall see him there."

"It is an odd whim."

"Hush! you know the people as well as I,

30

and he must please them," the other whispered. "He must conceal his power if he would live out his time. I will present you, and perhaps he may be gracious—ay, may even bid you to his banquet."

"A modest home," said young Vergilius.

Now they were nearing the palace of that mild and quiet gentleman whose name and title—Gaius Julius Cæsar Octavianus Augustus—had terrified the world; whose delicate hands flung the levin of his power to the far boundaries of India and upper Gaul, to the distant shores of Spain and Africa, and into deserts beyond the Euphrates.

"Many a poor patrician has better furniture and more servants and a nobler palace," said Appius. "Rather plain wood, divans out of fashion, rugs o'erworn; but you have seen them. He alone can afford that kind of thing."

"He has a fondness for old things."

"But not for old women, my dear fellow."

"Indeed! And he is himself sixty-one."

31

"Hist—the imperator! There, by the gate yonder."

An erect figure of a man rather above medium height, in a coarse, gray toga, stood by one of the white columns. Three Moorish children were playing about his knees, and a senator was talking with him.

"My public services are familiar to you," said the senator, as the young knights waited some twenty paces off. "A gift of two hundred thousand denarii would be fitting, and, if you will permit me to say so, it would delight the populace. Indeed, 'tis generally believed you have already given me a large sum."

"But see that you do not believe it," blandly spake the strange emperor, for albeit Rome was then a republic in name it was an empire in fact, and Augustus, wielding the power of an emperor, refused the title. Turning, he began to play with the children.

"Great and beloved father! I hope, at least, you will consider my prayer."

"Good senator, I have considered. You ask for two hundred thousand denarii. I can give you only the opportunity of earning them. As to myself, I am poor. Look at me. Even my time belongs to the people, and it is passing, my dear senator—it is passing."

The importunate man saw the subtle meaning in these words and went his way.

The emperor sat down, a child upon each knee, as the young men approached him. His head was bare and his fair, curly locks, growing low upon his forehead, were now touched with gray. He looked up at the two, his eyes blue, brilliant, piercing.

"My beloved Appius," said he, in a gentle tone, as he rose. "And this—let me think—ah, it is Vergilius, the son of Varro."

"It is wonderful you should remember me," said Vergilius.

"Wonderful? No. I could tell your age, your misdeeds, your virtues, and how often you failed to answer the roll-calls in Cappadocia. Well, I dare say they were pretty girls. But I forget; I am to-day seeking alms, my good children, for the poor of Rome. I am as ten thousand of the hungry standing before you here and asking for bread. In their name I shall receive, thankfully, what you may bestow."

Appius gave a handful of coins; Vergilius emptied his purse.

"'Tis not enough," said the latter. "Your words have touched me. To-night I shall send five thousand denarii to your palace."

"Well given, noble youth! It is generous. I like it in you. Say that I may have you to feast with me the first day before the ides—both of you. Say that I may have you."

"We humbly wait your commands," said Vergilius, kissing his hand.

"Now tell me, handsome son of Varro, have you found no pretty girl to your liking? Know you not, boy, 'tis time you married?" He held the hand of the young knight and spoke kindly, his cunning eyes aglow, and smiled upon him, showing his teeth, set well apart.

"Such an one I have found, good sire. Under the great purple dome there is none more beautiful, and with your favor and that of the gods I hope to make her my wife."

"Ah, then, I know her?"

"It is Arria, sister of Appius."

"And daughter of my beloved præfect. You are ambitious, my good youth."

The emperor stood a moment, looking downward thoughtfully. He felt his retreating chin. His smooth-shaven face, broad from bone to bone above the cheeks, quickly grew stern. His mind, which had the world for its toy and which planned the building or the treading down of empires, had turned its thought upon that little kingdom in the heart of the boy. And he was thinking whether it should stand or fall.

"It may be impossible," said he, turning to the young man. "Say no more to her until—until I have thought of it."

And Appius observed, as he went away with his friend: "You will be a statesman, my dear Vergilius; you gave him just the right dose of religion, flattery, and silver."

"I must succeed or I shall have no heart to live," said the other, soberly.

THAT evening Vergilius went to feast with the young Herodian prince, Antipater of Judea. The son of Herod was then a tall, swarthy, robust young man, who had come to see life in Rome and to finish his education. He would inherit the crown—so said they who knew anything of Herodian politics; but he was a Jew, and deep in the red intrigue of his father's house. So, therefore, he was regarded in Rome with more curiosity than respect. Augustus himself had said that he would rather be the swine of Herod than Herod's son, and he might have added that

37

he would rather be the swine of Antipater than his father. But that was before Augustus had learned that even his own household was unworthy of full confidence.

Antipater had brought many slaves to Rome, and some of the noblest horses in the empire. He had hired a palace and built a lion-house, where, before intimates, he was wont to display his courage and his skill. It had a small arena and was in the midst of a great garden. There he kept a lion from northern Africa, a tiger, and a black leopard from the Himalayas. He was training for the Herodian prize at the Jewish amphitheatre in Cæsarea. These great, stealthy cats in his garden typified the passions of his heart. If he had only fought these latter as he fought the beasts he might have had a better place in history.

Antipater had conceived a great liking for the sister of Appius. Her beauty had roused in him the great cats of passion now stalking their prey. He had sworn to his intimates that no other man should

38

marry her. His gallantry was unwelcome, he knew that, and Appius had assured him that a marriage was impossible; but the wild heart of the Idumean held to its purpose. And now its hidden eyes were gazing, catlike, on Vergilius, the cause of its difficulty. In Judea he would have known how to act, but in Rome he pondered.

It had been a stormy day in the palace of Antipater. He had crucified a slave for disobedience and run a lance through one of his best horses for no reason. He came out of his bath a little before the hour of his banquet, and two slaves, trembling with fear, followed him to his chamber. They put his tunic on him, and his sandals, and wound the fillets that held them in place. One of the slaves began brushing the dark hair of his master while the other was rubbing a precious ointment on his face and arms.

"Fool!" he shouted. "Have I not told you never to bear upon my head?"

He jumped to his feet, black eyes flash-

39

ing under heavy brows, and, seizing a lance, broke the slave's arm with a blow and drove him out of the chamber. A few minutes later, in a robe of white silk and a yellow girdle, he came into his banquet-hall with politeness, dovelike, worshipful, and caressing.

"Noble son of Varro!" said he, smiling graciously, "it is a joy to see you. And you, brave Gracus; and you, Aulus, child of Destiny; and you, my learned Manius; and you, Carus, favored of the Muses: I do thank you all for this honor."

It was a brilliant company—gay youths all, who could tell the new stories and loved to sit late with their wine. As they waited for dinner many tempting dishes were passed among them. There were oysters, mussels, spondyli, fieldfares with asparagus, roe-ribs, sea-nettles, and purple shell-fish. When they came to their couches, the dinner-table was covered with rare and costly things. On platters of silver and gold one might have seen tunny fishes from

40

Chalcedon, murænas from the Straits of Gades, peacocks from Samos, grouse from Phrygia, cranes from Melos. Slaves were kept busy bringing boar's head and sow's udder and roasted fowls, and fish pasties, and boiled teals. Other slaves kept the goblets full of old wine. Soon the banquet had become a revel of song and laughter. Suddenly Antipater raised a calix high above his head.

"My noble friends," he shouted, "I bid you drink with me to Arria, sister of Appius, and fairest daughter of Rome—"

Vergilius had quickly risen to his feet. "Son of Herod," said he, with dignity, "I am in your palace and have tasted of your meat, and am therefore sacred. You make your wine bitter when you mingle it with the name of one so pure. Good women were better forgotten at a midnight revel."

A moment of silence followed.

"My intention was pure as she," Antipater answered, craftily. "Be not so jealous,

my noble friend. I esteem her as the best
and loveliest of women."

"Nay, not the loveliest," said the young
Manius, an assessor in Judea. "I sing the
praise of Salome, sister of our noble prince.
Of all the forms in flesh and marble none
compare with this beautiful daughter of
the great king."

"May fairest women be for the best men,"
said Antipater, drinking his wine.

In a dim light along the farther side of
the dining-hall was a row of figures, some
draped, some nude, and all having the look
of old marble. Two lay in voluptuous at-
titudes, one sat on a bank of flowers, and
others stood upon pedestals.

There were all the varying forms of Venus
represented in living flesh. None, save
Antipater and the slaves around him, knew
that under each bosom was a fearful and
palpitating heart. They were beautiful
slave - girls captured on the frontiers of
Judea. In spite of aching sinew and
muscle, they had to stand like stone to

42

escape the observation of evil eyes. There was a cruelty behind that stony stillness of the maidens, equal, it would seem, to the worst in Hades.

Slaves kept the wine foaming in every goblet, and fought and danced and wrestled for the pleasing of that merry company, and the hours wore away. Suddenly the sound of a lyre hushed the revels. All heard the voice of a maiden singing, and turned to see whence it came. A sweet voice it was, trembling in tones that told of ancient wrong, in words full of a new hope. Had life and song come to one of those white marbles yonder? Voice and word touched the heart of Vergilius — he knew not why; and this in part is the chant that stopped the revels of Antipater:

" Lift up my soul; let me not be ashamed—I trust
    in Thee, God of my fathers;
  Send, quickly send, the new king whose arrows
    shall fly as the lightning,
  Making the mighty afraid and the proud to bow
    low and the wicked to tremble.

Soon let me hear the great song that shall sound
in the deep of the heavens;
Show me the lantern of light hanging low in
the deep of the heavens."

The voice of the singer grew faint and
the lyre dropped from her hands. They
could see her reeling, and suddenly she fell
headlong to the rug beneath her pedestal.
Antipater rose quickly with angry eyes.

"The accursed girl!" said he. "A Gal-
ilean slave of my father. She is forever
chanting of a new king."

Hot with anger and flushed with wine,
he ran, cursing, and kicked the shapely form
that lay fainting at the foot of its pedestal.

"Fool!" he shouted. "Know you not
that I only am your king? You shall be
punished; you shall enter the cage of the
leopard."

He went no further. Vergilius had rushed upon him and flung him to the floor.
Antipater rose quickly and approached the
young Roman, a devil in his eyes. Vergilius
had a look of wonder and self-reproach.

44

"What have I done?" said he, facing the Jew. "Son of Herod, forgive me. She is your slave, and I—I am no longer master of myself. I doubt not some strange god is working in me, for I seem to be weak-hearted and cannot bear to see you kick her."

The declaration was greeted with loud laughter. Antipater stood muttering as he shook the skirt of his toga.

" 'Tis odd, my good fellows," said Vergilius, "but the other day I saw a man scourging his lady's-maid. Mother of the gods! I felt as if the blows were falling on my own back, and out went my hand upon his arm and I begged him — I begged him to spare the girl."

All laughed again.

"You should have a doll and long hair," said Antipater, in a tone of contempt.

The proud son of Varro stood waiting as the others laughed, his brows and chin lifting a bit with anger. When silence came he spoke slowly, looking from face to face:

45

"If any here dare to question my courage, within a moment it shall be proved upon him."

None spoke or moved for a breath. Antipater answered, presently:

"I doubt not your courage, noble Vergilius, but if you will have it tried I can show you a better way, and one that will spare your friends. Come, all of you."

As they were rising, the young Gracus remarked: "By Apollo! I have not taken my emetic."

"To forget that is to know sorrow," said another.

Slaves brought their outer robes and they followed the young prince. He led them, between vines and fruit trees and beds of martagon and mirasolus, to the lion-house in his garden. Vergilius now understood the test of courage to be put upon him. The great beasts were asleep in their cages, and Antipater prodded them with a lance. A thunder in their throats seemed to fill the air and shake the flames in the lampadaria. With sword and lance Antipater entered the arena, a space barred high, about thirty feet square, upon which all the cages opened.

"The tiger!" he commanded.

Keepers lifted a metal gate, and the huge cat leaped away from their lances, backed snarling to the end of his cage, and with a slow, creeping movement put his head and fore-paws into the arena; then a swift step or two, a lowering of the great head, and side-long he stood, with eyes aglow and fangs uncovered, a low mutter in his mouth, like the roar of a mighty harp - string. Some fifteen feet away stood the son of Herod, his lance poised.

"Never strike while your beast has a foot to the ground," said he, keeping his gaze on the face of the tiger. "He will be quick to move and parry. Wait until he is in the air, and then thrust your lance."

He made a feint with his weapon; the tiger darted half his length aside, with a

47

great, bursting roar, and, crouching low, stealthily felt the ground beneath him.

"Watch him now," said the tall Antipater. "He will leap soon."

Again he drove him forward, and then the beast turned, facing his tormentor, and crouched low. There, in a huge setting of bone and muscle strangely fitted to its fierceness, with eyes of fire and feet of deadly stealth, its back arched like a drawn bow, the wild heart of the son of Herod seemed to be facing him.

"Look!" a slave shouted. "He has bent his bow."

The haired lip of the beast quivered; great cords of muscle were drawn tense. Like a flash the bow sprang and the columns of bone beneath him lifted, flinging his long, striped body in the air. With cat-like swiftness Antipater stepped aside, and while the huge beast was in mid-air, thrust the lance into his heart. He bore with all his strength and rushed away, seizing another weapon. The big cat fell and rose and struck

48

at the clinging lance, and stood a second flooding the floor with blood. Then down he went shuddering to his death. The young men shouted loud their applause in honor of Herod's son. While the beast was dying slaves came and sanded the floor. Then, presently, they swept up the red sand, and tying a rope to the legs of the limp tiger, dragged him away. They had done this kind of work before, and each knew his part. Presently Antipater called two of them.

"Bring that girl Cyran—she that chants of her new king," said he, as they ran to do his bidding.

"Noble prince, the strange god is again at work in me," said Vergilius, with rising ire. "I could not bear to see you put her with the leopard; I should rather face him myself."

"You!" said the other, tauntingly, and with a shrewd purpose. The youths turned to see if Vergilius would really accept the challenge. No man had ever faced a black.

leopard at close quarters without suffering death or injury.

"I," said Vergilius, promptly. "If it is amusement you desire, I can supply it as well as she. Surely I have more blood in me. If you wish only to feed the leopard — will I not make a better feast?"

A sound hushed them. It was the slave-girl, singing as she came near:

"Send, quickly send, the new king whose arrows
    shall fly as the lightning,
  Making the mighty afraid and the proud to bow
    low and the wicked to tremble.
  Soon let me hear the great song that shall sound
    in the deep of the heavens;
  Show me the lantern of light hanging low in
    the deep of the heavens."

She was fair to look upon as she came, led by the carnifex, her form, draped in soft, transparent linen, like that of a goddess in its outline, her face lighted even with that light of which she sang.

"The girl against a hundred denarii that

you cannot live an hour in the arena with him," said Antipater, hotly.

"I accept the wager," Vergilius calmly answered, laying off his robe and seizing a lance. He entered the arena and closed its gate behind him. "Drive the beast in upon me, son of Herod; and you, Gracus, be ready to hand me another lance."

The black leopard spat fiercely and struck at the points that were put upon it, the deep rumble in its throat swelling into loud crescendos. Of a sudden it bounded through the gateway and stood a moment, baring great fangs. The animal threatened with long hisses. Vergilius held its eye, his lance raised. The hissing ceased, the growl diminished, the stealthy paws moved slowly. Soon it rolled upon its side, purring, and seemed to caress the floor with head and paws — a trick to divert the gaze of Vergilius. The Satanic eyes were ever on its foe. As the beast lay there, twisting and turning, the black fur seemed to wrap it in the gloom of Tar-

tarus, and the fire of the burning lake to
shine through its eyes. While Vergilius
stood motionless and alert, a slave hurried-
ly entered the lion-house and spoke to Antipater.

"The imperator!" whispered the slave.
"He cannot wait; he must see you quickly."

"Where?"

"In the palace hall."

Antipater hurried away.

The slave-girl went close to the barred
arena.

"Young master," said she, in quick and
eager words, "the lamps are burning dim-
mer. They will go out soon. It is a trick.
You will not be able to see and the leopard
will rend you."

Antipater ran to the banquet-hall of his
palace, where sat the emperor, his chin resting thoughtfully on his hand. The great
Augustus did not look up nor even change
his attitude as the son of Herod came near
and bowed low and called him father.

"I have a plan," said the emperor.

thoughtfully, "—a pretty plan, my young prince of—of—"

"Judea?" suggested the young prince.

"Oh, well, it matters not," the great father went on. "You know that fair Vergilius, son of Varro? A headstrong, foolish youth he is, and I fear much that he is like to die shortly. What think you?"

The piercing eyes of Augustus were looking into those of the young man.

"My great father," said the latter, "I do not know."

"'Tis gross ignorance and unworthy of you," said Augustus, quickly, as he rose. "Well, I have bethought me of a pretty plan. Your funeral and his shall occur on the same day — a fine, great, amusing funeral," he added, thoughtfully. "It shall be so. Do not worry, I shall see you well buried. Ah, you are most impolite. Why do you not ask me to drink your health? My pretty prince, you look most ill and have need of my good wishes."

53

"Dominus!" said the other, trembling with anxiety.

"Dominus!" the old emperor shouted, angrily. "Call me ass, if you dare, but never call me 'Dominus.'"

"You honor me, great father," said the young man, his eyes staring with terror, "but I beg you to excuse me for a little time."

"Ah, so you would leave me," said the sly emperor, in his mildest tones. "A most inhospitable wretch, indeed."

The tall Jew was now pale with fright. His feeling showed in great beads of perspiration. He dared not to stay; he dared not to go. He was in a worse plight than Vergilius, now standing in the leopard's cage.

"A most inhospitable prince," the bland emperor repeated, smiling with amusement. "You are in a hurry?"

"I am ill."

The emperor stood smiling as Antipater glided away.

54

"Run, you knave!" said the former to himself, with a chuckle of satisfaction. "Upon my soul! the Jew has already set his snare."

Then the gentle and cunning man, Gaius Julius Cæsar Octavianus Augustus, made his way to the entrance where lecticarii were waiting with his litter.

"Can you hear the sound of running feet?" he inquired of the lady who sat beside him as they went away.

"Yes. What means it?"

He turned with a smile and a movement of his hand. Then he answered calmly:

"Death is chasing a man through the garden yonder."

While Antipater was running towards the lion-house, that small tragedy of the arena was near its end.

The lights are burning low. Two have flickered for a little and gone out. The young men are watching with eager eyes.

"I can bear it no longer," says one, rushing to the gate of the arena, only to find that he could not open it.

The slave-girl utters a cry and steps forward and is caught and held by the carnifex.

Vergilius urges the leopard. He steps quickly, feinting with his lance; the cat darts along the farther side of the arena, roaring. Its eyes glow fiery in the dusk. The beast is become furious with continued baiting. Half the lamps are out and the light rapidly failing as Antipater rushes through the door. He falls beside the arena, rises and opens the gate.

"A lance," he whispers, and it is quickly put in his hands. "Come, come quickly, son of Varro," he whispers again. "The light is failing. He will tear you into shreds. Come through the gate here."

Vergilius had stopped, facing the leopard with lance raised.

"Not unless I have the wager," says he, calmly.

"You have won it," Antipater answers.

56

"Come, good friend, be quick, I beg of you!"

Both moved backward through the gate, and before it closed there came a fling of claws on the floor. A black ball, bound hard with tightened sinew, rose in the air and shot across the arena and shook the gate which had closed in time to stop it.

"You are living, son of Varro, and I thank the God of my fathers," Antipater shouted, as he flung himself on a big divan, his breath coming fast. "I forgot the lights. I thought of them suddenly, and ran to save you. If I had been running in the games I should have won the laurel of Cæsar."

"I was wrong—he could not have meant to slay me," thought Vergilius. "Not by the paws of the leopard."

Cyran stood near the door, weeping. Antipater rose and led her to Vergilius.

"The girl is yours," said he. "I am glad to be done with her. Come, all."

They followed him to the palace, and

Vergilius bade the girl dress and be ready to join his pedisequi in the outer hall. She knelt before him and kissed the border of his tunic.

"Oh, my young master!" said she, "I shall be of those who part the briers in your way." Then she hurried to obey him.

"I would speak with you, noble son of Varro," said Antipater, beckoning.

Vergilius followed to the deep atrium of the palace, where they stood alone.

"You have one thing I desire, and I will pay you five thousand aurei to relinquish it—five thousand aurei," the Jew whispered.

"And what is it you would buy of me, noble prince?"

"A mere plaything! A bouquet that will fade shortly and be flung aside. The thing happens to suit my fancy, and—and I can afford it."

In the moment of silence that followed this remark a stern look of inquiry came into the face of Vergilius.

"Man, do you not know? 'Tis the sister of Appius," Antipater added, lightly.

"Cur of Judea!" hissed the knight, his sword flashing out of its scabbard, "I shall cut you down and fling you out to the dogs. Fight here and now. I demand it!"

The young Roman spoke loudly and stood waiting. Those others had heard the challenge and were now coming near. Antipater stood silent, glaring, as had the leopard, with an evil leer at his foe, and thinking no doubt of the warning of Augustus. The stiff, straight hairs in his mustache quivered as he turned slowly, watchfully, towards the others, who were now standing near. Since his funeral should occur on the same day, how could he fight with Vergilius?

"You dare not," the latter added, fiercely; "and before these men I denounce you as a coward—a coward who fears to raise a hand."

His arm was extended, his finger at the

face of the Jew, now white with passion. Half a moment passed in which there was no word.

"You living carrion!" said the young knight, turning and walking away. "I am done with you."

He took the hand of the poor slave Cyran, and walked to the farther side of the atrium. He turned, still white with anger as if unsatisfied.

"Pet of harlots!" said he, fiercely. "It is time for some one to stand for the honor of good women. If you do but speak her name again before me I will run you through."

Receiving no answer, he departed with Cyran, while the others gathered about their host.

There was a heavy rumble in the throat of Antipater—a tiger-like, Herodian trait— and then a volley of oaths came out of it. He trembled with rage and flung his sword far across the dim atrium with a shout of anger. Like the great cats in his rage, he was like them also in his methods of attack —sly and terrible, but with a deep regard for the integrity of his own skin. Sure of his advantage, he could be as brave as when he faced the tiger.

He sat awhile muttering, his face between his hands. Soon, having calmed his passion, he rose and snarled: "Good sirs, never quarrel with the pet of an emperor, for if one spares you the other will not."

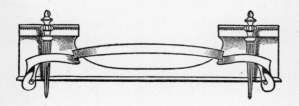

RRIA and her mother sat with the emperor. He was at home and in a playful humor. The hour of his banquet was approaching. Soon he would be summoned to receive his guests.

"Nay, but I am sure he loves me," the girl was saying.

The cunning emperor smiled and spoke very gently. "Think you so, dear child? I will put him to the test. Soon we shall know if he be worthy of so great a prize. I will try both his wit and his devotion, but you—you cannot be here."

"And why, great father?"

"Think you it could be a test with your eye upon him?"

"Oh, but I must see it," said the girl. "Unless I see it I shall not know. Let me be your slave and stand behind you in gray cloth. Beloved father, I implore you, let me see the test."

"Ah, well," said the emperor, rising, with a smile. "I shall know nothing but that you have gone above-stairs to find Clia, mistress of the robes. Tell her to give you a box of tablets, and when I raise my finger — so — they are to be delivered. Away with you."

Arria left with a cry of joy, and presently Augustus went with the Lady Lucia to meet his guests.

The "commands" of the emperor had given the hour of the banquet and prescribed the dress to be worn. Vergilius had waited anxiously for the moment when he should again see the great god of Rome, who could give or take away as he would. Standing at the door of Cæsar, he wondered whether he were nearing the end of all pleasure or the gate of paradise.  A plate of polished brass hung on its lintel, bearing in large letters the word *Salve*.  A slave opened the door and took his pallium.  Julia, that wayward daughter of Augustus, now three times married but yet beautiful, met him in the inner hall, and together they walked to the banquet-room.  There the emperor, limping slightly, came to meet Vergilius, and there, also, were the guests, seven in number: Appius and his mother, the Lady Lucia; Terentia, wife of the late Mæcenas; Manius, an assessor in Judea; Hortensius, legate of Spain; Antipater, son of Herod the Great; and Aulus Valerius Maro, the senator.

"It enters my thought to say to you," said the emperor, aside, as he put his hand upon the shoulder of Vergilius, "keep the number one in your mind, so that by-and-by you can tell me what you make of it."

Slaves had covered the table with fish and fowl in dishes of unwrought silver. The guests reclined upon three great divans

64

set around as many sides of the table.
They ate resting on their elbows, and were
so disposed that each could see the host
without turning. The emperor asked only
for coarse bread, a morsel of fish, two
figs, and a bit of cheese.

"My good friends," said he, in a low
voice, when the wine was served, "we have
with us an able officer in this young Manius,
one of our assessors in Jerusalem. I ask
you to drink his health. Though I can
drink no wine, I can feel good sentiments."

One could not help remarking his fixed
serenity of face and voice and manner as he
went on:

"Some time ago it came to my ear that
he thought me a tyrant wallowing in vulgar
and ill-gotten luxury."

There was a little stir in those heads
around the table, and in every hand and
face one might have seen evidence of quick-
ened pulses. The young officer was now
staring through deathly pallor.

"My friends, it is not strange," said the

great Augustus, mildly. "To Jerusalem
is quite two thousand miles; and, then,
he was very young when he left the
home of his fathers. Am I not right,
Manius?"

"Your words are both true and kindly,"
said the young man.

"And you are discerning," said the emperor, with a smile. "Now, good people, observe that I have invited our young officer
to Rome for two purposes: to show him,
first, that I live no better than the poorest
nobleman; secondly, that I am only a ser-
vant of the people; for, since he is an able
officer, I shall resist my own will and keep
him in the public service."

"Bravo!" said they all, and clapped their
hands.

A strange, inscrutable man was the emperor at that moment, the mildness of a
lamb in his voice and manner, the gleam
of a serpent's eye under his brows. And
that right hand of his, clinched now and
quivering a little, had it grasped a reach-

ing, invisible serpent within him? Kindly?
Yes, but with the kindness of a deep and
subtle character who saw in forbearance the
best politics and the most effective disci-
pline. Lights were now aglow in a great
candelabrum over the table and in many
tall lampadaria.

A slave, who was a juggler, came near
and began to fill the gloom above him
with golden disks. From afar came the
music of flutes and timbrels. Julia retired
presently, and returned soon with her pet
dwarf Cenopas. She stood him on a large,
round table, and the guests greeted him
with loud laughter as he looked down.
He had a hard, unlovely face, that little
dwarf. He suggested to Vergilius unwelcome thoughts of a new sort of Cupid—de-
formed, evil, and hideous — typifying the
degenerate passions of Rome. There were
in the quiver of this Cupid arrows which
carried the venom of the asp. Some at the
table mocked his grinning face and made a
jest of his deformity. When he could be

heard he mimicked the speech and manners of public men.

"A Cupid with a knot in his back," said one.

"And if I were to aim an arrow at you," said the dwarf, quickly, "I'm sure you'd have a pain in yours."

"My dear," said the gentle-mannered emperor, when the laughter had died away, "I think we shall now give him the crown of folly and let him go."

"Between the greatest and the least of Romans," said his daughter, rising and pointing at her father and then at the dwarf, "I am lost in mediocrity."

A slave took the little creature in his arms and bore him away as if he had been a pet dog.

"Tell me, young men," said the emperor, "have you no lines to read us— you that have youth and beauty and sweethearts? How is it with you, good Vergilius?"

The young man shook his head. "No,"

68

said he; "I have youth and a sweetheart, but not the gift of poesy."

"No lines! What are we coming to in this Rome of ours? Are there no more poets? My dear friends, tell me, in the baths or the forum or the theatre, or wherever the people congregate, do you hear of no youth that has the divine gift of song?"

He paused for a little, but there was no reply.

"Then Rome is in evil days," said the great father, sadly.

"Why?" It was the question of Gracus.

"Why, young man? Because in every land there should be those who can cherish the fear of the gods and make honor beautiful and love sacred and valor a thing of imperishable fame. I assure you, good people, one poet is better," he paused, thoughtfully — "than ten thousand soldiers," he added. "Who will bring me a poet?"

The gods are indeed helpless, thought Vergilius. They must have poets to do their work for them? But he said nothing.

69

"The streets are full of poets," said Gracus.

"Those old men with long beards and stilted rubbish!" said Augustus, "with tragedies that slay the hero and the hearer! Bring me a poet, and, remember, I shall honor him above all men. Once I invited Horace to dine with me, and got no answer. He was a proud man"—this with a merry smile. "Again I invited him, and then he deigned to write me a sentence, merely, and said: 'Thanks, I am happy out here on my farm.' I did not know what to do, but I wrote a letter and said to the great man: 'You may not desire my friendship, but that is no reason for my failing to value yours.' I am proud to say that he was my friend ever after. But I weary you."

A female slave, thickly veiled, stood behind him. He made a signal and she quickly put in his hand a little box of ivory, finely wrought.

"I have here," said the great father,

"nine disks of wax. You see they are very small, but so they shall serve my purpose the better. Will each of you take one and retire from the table and write upon it the thing he most desires? Now, my dear friends, brevity is ever as the point of the lance. Wit is blunt and Truth half armed without it. I lay a test upon you."

All retired quickly, and, soon returning, dropped their wishes in the box. The playful emperor closed and shook it and withdrew a disk.

"I find here the word 'preference,'" said he, and all observed that his keen eyes were calmly measuring the prince Antipater. "It is a poor word, and does you little honor, my young friend. In mere preference there is no merit. Here is another, and it says 'more wine.' Keep his goblet full," he added, pointing to that of the senator, as all laughed. "Here is one says 'rest.' Have patience, my good daughter, I shall soon be done talking. Another has on it the words 'your health'—a charming compli-

71

ment, dear Lady Lucia. 'Courage,' 'wisdom,' 'success,'" he added, reading from the tablets. "Naturally, and who, indeed, does not desire those things? Here is one that says 'help'—a great word, upon my soul! He that prays for help and not for favor, if he do his best, may have many good things—even 'courage,' 'wisdom,' 'success.' Keep at work and you shall have my help, Appius, and, I doubt not, that of the gods also. Here is one—I like it best of all—it is that of the modest young Vergilius. He would have a priceless thing. And do you," he inquired, turning to the young knight, "desire this above all things? Think; there is the distinction of place and power and honor — the ring of a legate would become you well!"

"But, above all," said Vergilius, "I desire that I have written."

"Beautiful boy!" said the cunning emperor. "'Tis so great a prize, give me another test of your quality. With one word you ask for one thing. To try your wit, I give you a theme so small it is next to naught — the number one. Tell us, and briefly as you may, what is in it."

The young man rose and bowed low. "One is in all numbers," said he, "and unless all numbers are as one they are nothing. I desire one mistress for my heart, one purpose for my conduct, and one great master for my country."

"The gods grant them!" said Augustus, leading the applause.

"And now I shall proclaim the word he has written. It is 'Arria,' and stands, I know well, for the sister of Appius."

He turned quickly to the still and silent figure of the slave behind him. All eyes were now watching her.

"Are you content?" he inquired.

Gray veil and robe fell away, revealing the beautiful sister of Appius. Vergilius went quickly to her side.

"I declare them for each other!" said the emperor, as all rose and gathered around the two. He took the boy's hand.

"Come to me at ten to-morrow," he added.

"But, O father of Rome!" said Arria, looking up at the great man, "how long shall you detain him?"

"Give me half an hour, you love-sick maiden," said Augustus. "He shall be at your palace in good time."

"Come at the middle hour," said the Lady Lucia, her hand upon the arm of Vergilius.

"The gods give you sleep," said the great father, as he bade them good-night.

Beneath the laurels on their way to the gate, Gracus, who rode with Antipater, said:

"And what of your oath, son of Herod?"

"But they are not yet married," the other answered, malevolently. "Vergilius! Bah! He is the son of a prætor and I am the son of a king. Curse the old fox! He never spoke to me after greetings, and once when I glanced up at him I

74

thought his keen eyes were looking through me."

"Those eyes! Jupiter!" said Gracus, "they drop a plummet into one."

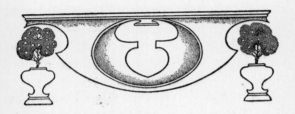

# Chapter

## 6

NOW there were few barriers between the emperor and the people. He went to work in his study at an early hour and gave a patient hearing to any but foolish men. This morning he had been reading a long address from the legate of Syria. He had a way of dividing his thought between reading and small affairs of the state. His legate recited all he had been able to learn of the new king they were now expecting in Judea. He told also of a plot which had baffled all his efforts and which aimed to take the life of Herod and crown the king of prophecy and divine power.

"We must have a spy of noble blood and bearing, of unswerving fidelity and honor, and with some knowledge of the religion of Judea," said the legate. "Of course, you will not be able to find him, for where in all the world, save yourself, good father, is there such a man?"

Augustus dropped the sheet of vellum and rubbed his chin thoughtfully.

"How about this young Vergilius—the handsome, clever, woman-loving Vergilius?" he thought. Then for a moment the cunning emperor laughed silently.

Ever since he began to read the letter he had been conversing with his daughter Julia.

"If you can propose a better candidate for the girl, I—" he paused, looking intently at the letter—"I shall consider him," he added, presently.

"She is beautiful," his daughter whispered. "I know one who will give to the state many thousand aurei."

"No need of hurry. The young Vergilius

will give what is better than money, and then—"

The emperor paused again.

"And then?" it was the inquiry of Julia.

"He will forget her and she will grow weary and yield. There's time enough, and time"—he took a little mirror from the table and looked down upon it—"can accomplish many things," he added. "It will have the assistance of fame and honor and new faces. Now go, I beg of you, and leave me to my work."

A delegation of Jews—petty merchants of the Trastevere — were leaving as Vergilius entered. The emperor, now alone save for his young caller, rose and gave him a sprig of laurel.

"Sit here," said he, resuming his seat and pausing for a little to study a sheet of vellum in his hands. He continued, without raising his eyes: "I have another test for you, my fair son. You shall be assistant procurator in Jerusalem, with rank of tribune.

It may be you shall have command of the castle. Three days from now take the south road with Manius and a troop of horse. This court of Herod—of course, I am speaking kindly, my dear Vergilius—but, you may know, it is a place of mysteries, and there are many things I do not need to *say* to *you*."

The old emperor, leaning forward, touched the arm of the young man and gave him a cunning glance.

"A cipher," he added, passing the sheet of vellum. "It will be known to you and to me only. You will understand what I wish to know. You shall have command of a cohort."

Vergilius thought for a second of that strange overhauling of Manius the night before, and of the shrewdness of the great father in returning him, kindly, to his task, with a pair of eyes to keep watch of him.

"With all my heart I thank you," said the young knight. "But — my beloved father—I was hoping to marry and—and know the path of peace."

"But I am sure you will wait two years—only two years," said the other, rising with extended hands. "There is time enough; and remember, whether to peace or war, your path is that of duty. Farewell!"

It was a way he had of commanding, kindly but inexorable, and Vergilius knew it. Again he spoke as the knight turned away.

"This young Antipater—do you know him?"

"Not well."

"But, possibly, well enough," said the emperor, with a knowing look. Then, casually: "Oh, there is yet a little matter—that new king the Jews are looking for—if he should come, I suppose he will report to me, but—but let me know what you learn. Study the Jewish faith and discover what this hope is founded upon." Then he turned quickly and went away.

This "little matter" counted much with the shrewd emperor. Kings were his puppets, and if there were to be a new one he must, indeed, consider what to do with him. Yet he had shame of his interest in "that foolish gossip" of an alien race. Therefore he put it only as a trifling afterthought. But he had a way of talking with his eyes, and the alert youth read them well.

That elation of the young lover now had its boundary of thoughtfulness. Going down the Palatine, he was also descending his hill of happiness. Below him, in the Forum, he could see the golden mile-stone of Augustus, now like a pillar of fire in the sunlight; he could see the beginning of those many roads radiating from it to far peripheries of the empire. Tens of thousands had turned their backs upon it, leaving with slow feet, some to live in distant, inhospitable lands, some to die of fever and the sword, some to return forgotten of their kindred, and some few with laurels of renown; but all of these many who went away were leaving, for long or forever, love and home and peace.

"The army is sucking our blood, and Hate grows while Love is starving," Vergilius reflected, as he went along, while a hideous, unwelcome thought grew slowly, creeping over him. This golden mile-stone was the centre of a great spider-web laced by road and sea way to the far corners of the empire; and that cunning, alert man—who was he but the spider?

"And I—what am I, now, but one of his flies caught in the mighty web?" he thought. "Love and its peace have come to me and I shall know them—for three days—and perhaps no longer."

His wealth and rank and influence might, if used with diplomacy, have kept him at home, for, after all, he was a Varro; but Arria had been used to press him into bondage.

"Another test!" he said to himself. "Ah,

what a cunning old fox! He needed a spy,
and one of character and noble blood.
How well he tested my cleverness! And
now I am his, body and soul."

# Chapter

7

HILE Vergilius, going slowly, was thinking of these things, Vanity, the only real goddess who, in Rome, managed the great theatre of fashion, had her stage set for a love scene. It was to occur in the triclinium, or great banquet-hall, of a palace — that of the Lady Lucia. There were portrait-masks and mural paintings on either wall; ancestral statues of white marble stood in a row against the red wall; there were seats and divans of ebony enriched by cunning hands; lamp-holders of wrought metal standing high as a man's head, and immense violet rugs on the floor.

84

The heroine wore a white robe banded low with purple, and her jewelled hair was in fillets of gold. There was always a pretty artfulness in the match-making of a patrician beauty and her mother. Indeed, life had grown far from elemental emotions.

"Now, when he enters," said the girl, turning to the Lady Lucia, "I shall bring him here at once and sit down by this heap of cushions, and then—Oh, god of my heart! What shall I do with that big man—what shall I say to him?"

"My dear, he will speak, and then you will know what to say," said the matron. "Only do not let him know that you love him—at least, not for a time yet."

"Too late; I fear he knows it now—the wretch!" said Arria, rubbing her cheeks to make them glow.

"But mind you hold him off, and do not let him caress you for an hour at least. One kiss and one only."

"One!" the girl repeated, with contempt. "How ungenerous are the old!"

85

"Hard to count are a lover's kisses," her mother answered, with a sigh. "But you can use them up in a day. Really, you can use them up all in a day."

"A day full of kisses! Oh, heart of me! Think of it!" said the beautiful girl, covering her face a moment. "I will not have the yellow cushions," she added, quickly. "Here, take these and bring me two violet ones, and that cushion of gauze filled with rose leaves. I will have that in my lap when we are sitting here. Now what do you think of the colors?" she demanded.

"Beautiful! And best of all that in your cheeks. I doubt not he will worship you."

"Or he is no kind of a man," said Arria, thoughtfully. "Oh, son of Varro! come, I am waiting. If he takes me in his arms, what shall I do?"

"Thrust him aside—tell him that you do not like it."

"And what shall I do if he does not?"

"Bid him go at once. We have no need of any half-men."

"But he will," said the girl, with a worried look. "He shall embrace me—he shall, or—or I will bid my brother kill him. Oh, wretch!" She jumped to her feet with a merry cry. "I have an idea," she added, clapping her hands. "When the sunlight falls on the floor yonder, I will get up and dance in it."

"A pretty trick!" said her mother.

"Oh, son of Varro! why do you not come?" said the girl, impatiently. "I love him so I could die for him—I could die for him! Perhaps he loves me not and I shall never see him again."

She hurried to the outer court, whispering anxiously: "Come, son of Varro. Oh, come quickly, son of Varro!"

When Vergilius arrived Arria was waiting for him there in the court of the palace. Her white silk rustled as she ran to meet him. Her cheeks had the pink of roses and her eyes a glow in them like that of diamonds. She stopped as he came near, and turned away.

'Tears?" said he, leaning down, with his arms about her. "Oh, love, let me see your face!"

She turned quickly with a little toss of her head and took a step backward.

"You shall not call me love," said she— "not yet. You have not told me that you love me."

"I told all who were at the palace of the great father."

"But you have not told me, son of Varro."

"I do love you." He was approaching.

"Hush! Not now," she answered, taking his hand in hers—temporizing. "Come, I will race with you."

She ran, leading him, with quick, pattering feet through an inner hall and up the long triclinium. There, presently, she threw herself upon the heap of cushions.

"Now, sit," said she, draping her robe and then feeling her hair that was aglow with jewels.

A graceful and charming creature was this child of the new empire, a noble beauty

in her face and form, the value of a small
kingdom on her body. "Not so near," said
she, as he complied. "Now, son of my
father's friend, say what you will and
quickly."

"I love you," he began to say.

"Wait," she whispered, stopping him as
she turned, looking up and down the great
hall. "It is for me alone. I will not share
the words with any other. Now tell me—
tell me, son of Varro," she whispered, moving nearer; "tell me at once."

"I love you, sweet girl, above gods and
men. You are more to me than crowns of
laurel and gold, more than all that is in the
earth and heavens. My heart burns when
I look at you."

He hesitated, pressing her hand upon his
lips.

"Is that all?" said she, with a pretty sad-
ness, looking down at the golden braces on
her fan. "Now, say it again, all, slowly."

She might as well have told a bird how
he should sing.

He went on all unconscious of her command, his words lighted by the fire in his heart. They were as waters rippling in the sun-glow.

"Without you there is no light in the heavens, no beauty in the earth, no hope or glory in the future, no joy in my heart. My sword threatens me, dear love, when I think of losing you."

She turned, quickly, with almost a look of surprise.

"It is beautiful," said she, with a sigh; "but is there no more? Think, dear, noble knight; do think of more!"

She was near forgetting her plan. He took her in his arms and kissed her.

"Think—think of more," said she, "and I will dance the tourina."

There was a note of gladness in her voice. It rang merry as a girdle of silver bells. Now, on the floor near them was a golden square of sunlight, and, tabret in hand, she sprang up and began to dance in it. She moved swiftly back and forth, her arms extended, her white robe flowing above the sapphires in each purple fillet on her ankles

"Now, dear Vergilius, tell me, why do you love me?" she said, throwing herself upon the cushions near him with glowing cheeks.

"Because you are Arria. Because Arria is you. Because I must, for your pure and noble heart and for your beauty," said he. "When I look upon you I forget my dreams of war and conquest; I think only of peace and love and have no longer the heart to slay. Oh, sweet Arria! I feel as if I should fling my swords into the Tiber."

"Oh, my love! could I make you throw your swords into the Tiber I should be very happy." Her eyes had turned serious and thoughtful. Her girlish trickery had come to an end. Vanity retired, now, and Love had sole command.

He put his arms about her and rained kisses upon her face, her hair, her eyes.

"Say it all again, dear Vergilius—say it a hundred times," she whispered.

"My dear one, I love you more than I can say. Now am I prepared to speak in deeds, in faithfulness, in devotion."

"But, once more, why do you love me? Why me?" said she, moving aside with an air of preoccupation, her chin resting upon her hand, her elbow upon the gauze pillow of rose leaves in her lap. "Is it my beauty more than myself?"

"No," he answered; "your beauty is intoxicating, and I thank the gods for it, but your sweet self, your soul, is more, far more to me than your grace and all your loveliness."

She had dreamed of such love but never hoped for it, and now all the pretty tricks she had thought of had become as the mummery of fools. She sat in silence for a little space, her eyes upon her girdle, and a new and serious look came into her face.

"I shall try, then," said she, presently—

"I shall try to be noble. But shall you— shall you truly throw your swords into the Tiber?"

"Would I might," said he, sadly. "And now I must tell you—" He paused, and Arria turned quickly, her lips trembling as her color faded.

"In three days I go to Jerusalem," he added, "by command of the emperor."

"For how long?" she whispered, her eyes taking years upon them as the seconds flew.

"For two years."

Quickly she hid her face in the cushions and her body quivered. That old, familiar cry, which had in it the history and the doom of Rome, rang in the great halls around them — that cry of forsaken women.

"The iron foot is upon us," said he. "Do not let it tread you down as it has other women. Be my vestal and guard the holy fire of love."

Then he told of Cyran, the slave-girl, and added: "I leave her in your care. Every day she will cause you to think of me."

# Chapter
## 8

T was near the middle hour of the night. Many, just out of banquet-hall, theatre, and circus, thronged the main thoroughfares of the capital. Cries of venders, ribald songs, shouts of revelry, the hurrying of many feet roused the good people who, wearied by other nights of dissipation, now sought repose. They turned, uneasily, reflecting that to-morrow they would have their revenge.

Antipater had dined with but a single guest—a young priest, who, arriving that very day from Damascus, had sought the palace of his countryman. The service at

95

his table had not pleased the prince. Leaping from his couch, he struck down a slave and ordered his crucifixion. It was a luckless Arab, who many times had unwittingly offended his master.

Now the son of Herod lay asleep where, a little time ago, he had been feasting. Manius, who had just entered the palace of his friend, came into the banquet-hall. He touched the arm of Antipater, who started with a curse and rose with an apology.

"I was dreaming of foes and I see a friend," he muttered. "Forgive me, noble Manius."

The prince pulled a golden bell-cord that shone against the green pargeting of the wall.

"Now to our business," he whispered, turning to the officer.

They crossed the atrium, descended a stairway, and threw open a barred door. They were now in a gloomy passage between walls of marble. Antipater halted, pres-

ently, and tapped with his seal ring on a
metal door. Then a rattle of bolts and the
door swung open.

"Now," Antipater whispered, "are you of
the same mind?"

"I am."

"And again you swear secrecy?"

"I do."

Without more delay they entered a room
walled with white marble and lighted by
candles. A bearded Jew, in a scarlet
cloak embroidered with gold, rose to greet
them.

"To John ben Joreb I present the noble
Manius," said Antipater.

"Blessings of the one God be upon thee,"
said Ben Joreb, bowing low.

"And the favor of many gods on thee,"
said the assessor. "From Jerusalem?"

"Nay, from Damascus."

Antipater stirred the fire in iron braziers
on either side of the room, and then bade
them recline beside him at a small table
whereon a supper waited.

"Ben Joreb has good news of our plan," said he, turning to Manius.

"It prospers," said the priest. "Our council is now in thirty cities."

"And the king is better," said Manius. "He will not soon perish of infirmity."

"But you tell me that my father suffers?"

Antipater started nervously. A long, weird wail from the Arab dying on a cross in the garden flooded down the flues.

"A hundred deaths a day," said Ben Joreb.

"I have been talking with Manius," Antipater answered. "He thinks it would be a mercy to—"

He was interrupted again. That tremulous, awful cry for mercy found its way to his ear. It seemed to mock the sacred word. Antipater jumped to his feet, cursing.

"I will put an end to that," said he, rushing to the door and flinging it back and running down the passage.

Manius turned to Ben Joreb.

"What is there in the howling of that slave?" he whispered. "I am weak-hearted."

"I take it for a sign," the other answered, gravely. "It is written, 'Thy spirit shall be as the candle of the Lord,' and, again, 'Thou shalt hearken to the cry of anguish.'"

In a few moments Antipater returned.

"I have summoned the carnifex," said he, bolting the door and resuming his place at the table. "I was saying to you, good Manius, that my friend here, Ben Joreb, would think it a great mercy to remove him."

"A great mercy!" Ben Joreb answered; "a man's mercy to him; a God's mercy to his people."

"And what think you?" said Antipater, turning to Manius.

"I agree; 'twould be a mercy, but a risky enterprise," said the Roman.

"I would risk my head to save him a day of pain," said the treacherous son of Herod.

"You love him not as I do or you would brave all to end his misery."

There was now half a moment filled with a long, piercing cry from beyond the walls of the palace until Antipater spoke, a tiger look in his face again. "Put the lance into him, my good carnifex," he growled, striking with clinched fist. "Again, now; and again, and again."

He listened for a breath, and as silence came he added, "There, that will do."

Neither spoke for a little time.

"I wish I could make you feel how dearly I love my father," he went on, addressing his friends now and hiding his claws with revolting guile and all unconscious that he had shown them.

Again a breath of silence, in which Manius thought of the black leopard when he lay making those playful and caressing movements on the floor. And there came to the heart of Ben Joreb a fear that this man might prove more terrible than his father.

"We feel it," said Manius, with inner smiles that showed not upon his face.

"Then be servants of my love."

"And of our own welfare?"

"Certainly! You shall each have a palace in Jerusalem and fifty thousand aurei; and you, Manius, shall command the forces on land and sea, and you, John ben Joreb, of the tribe of Aaron, shall be high-priest."

"I agree," said Manius, an overwhelming cupidity in the words.

"And I agree," said the Jew, who had entered upon this intrigue with motives of patriotism, and now, although suspicious of the result, was committed beyond a chance of turning.

"Angels of mercy!" Antipater exclaimed, rising and taking a hand of each in his. "My love shall be ever a shield and weapon for you. One other thing. The couriers who bring to Rome news of my father's death—bid them hurry and take with them, also, word of the illness of that dog Vergilius. After they leave let him not linger in needless pain—do you understand me? For that, I say, each of you shall have five thousand aurei added to his wealth."

The others nodded.

"Now take this—it may be useful," whispered the prince of Judea, handing a little golden box to the assessor. "There is something in it will hasten the effect of wine — a fine remedy for a weary land, good Manius. He that makes it a friend shall have no enemies. Hold, let me think. That old fox on the hill yonder has a thousand eyes and his ears are everywhere. Not a word, Manius, after we leave this door. In yon passage turn to the right. Walk until your head touches the ceiling, then creep to the door. Open it and use your ears. If no one is passing, go straight ahead. You will come to a gate on the Via Sacra. You," he added, turning to Ben Joreb, "shall leave by the main gate."

When both had gone, this prince of Judea walked across the inner hall of his palace and flung himself on the cushions of a great divan.

A swarthy eunuch came near him on tiptoe.

"Begone!" The word burst from the lips of Antipater in a hoarse growl, and, like a tiger's paw, his hand struck the cushions in front of him. As he lay blinking drowsily, his chin upon his hands, there was still in his face and attitude a suggestion of the monster cat.

And he thought fondly of his wreaking of vengeance when he should be crowned the great king of prophetic promise—of the fury of armies, of the stench of the slain, of the cry of the ravished, of "mountains melting in blood."

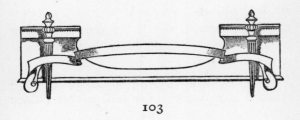

## Chapter

9

IT was the fifth anniversary of that resolution of the senate fathers to consecrate the altar of Peace. Pilgrims thronged the city, and some had journeyed far. Tens of thousands surrounded the great monument, immense and beautiful beyond any in the knowledge of men. It signalized a remarkable state of things —the world was at peace. More than seven centuries before that day an idea had entered the heart of a prophet; now it was in the very heart of the world. This heap of marble, under pagan gods, had given it grand, if only partial, expression. There was no symbol of war in the long procession of its upper frieze, and its lower was like a sculptured song of peace wrought in fruits and bees and birds and blossoms. Here was a mighty plant flowering twice a year and giving its seed to the four winds. Every July and January its erection was celebrated in the imperial republic.

Vergilius stood beside the emperor that day when, at the Ars Pacis Augustæ, he addressed the people.

"I have been reading," he said, "the words of a certain dreamer of Judea, who, in the olden time, wrote of a day when swords should be beaten into ploughshares and spears into pruning-hooks, and when peace should reign among the nations of the earth. Well, give me an army for a hundred years, good people, and then I may voice the will of the gods that iron be used no more to plough its way in living flesh, but only to turn the furrow and to prune the tree. Meanwhile, believe me, every man must learn to love honor and virtue, and to respect his neighbor, and the gods above all."

A hundred years! The playful emperor knew not how quickly a man passes and how slowly, how exceeding slowly, moves the great procession of mankind. But so it befell; the very right hand of Jupiter had helped in the sowing of that seed which, as it grew, was to lift the foundations of his power.

Vergilius left the scene with Augustus. They rode away in the royal litter.

"In all the great cities men are speaking to-day of the value of peace and honor," said the subtle emperor—a sceptic in religion, a cynic in philosophy, a rake in private life, and a conqueror who commanded "peace" with a trained army of four hundred and fifty thousand men.

"It is a great thing to do," said the young knight.

"Give me men enough to say it, and if they grow not weary I will bring the world to believe that the sun is only the breast-

plate of Jupiter," said Augustus. "Honor
and peace are good things—do not forget
that, my young friend. Give the words to
your tongue, not flippantly, but with a sober
eye, and often, my brave knight — often.
You leave to - morrow — have you made
ready?"

"Ready but for the leave-taking;" this
with a sigh.

"It ill becomes you to be cast down.
Shake your heart with laughter—it will roll
away the stone of regret. Buy a fool, my
young friend. For five thousand denarii
you may obtain a most excellent fool."

He knew the price of all, from the hewer
of wood to the crowned king, but only he
could afford a slave like that.

"I should prefer a wise man," said the
young knight.

"Philosophers are more expensive," the
father continued, craftily—"twenty thousand denarii, and dear at that. They will
teach you little but discontent. I recom-
mend a grammarian."

107

The old emperor turned his cunning eyes upon the face of Vergilius.

"Forty thousand, at least, for a good one," he added; "but a youth of your talent should remember the value of immortal fame." Word and look were a hint to the young man that he should prepare himself with all diligence for an active career in the senate. The youth understood their meaning and was a trifle comforted. There was no promise nor the least warrant for a claim —it was only the emperor's way of guiding.

They were now passing a row of shops on the Via Claudia. The emperor, putting his hand out of the door, motioned to his lecticarii and they halted.

"Come with me," said the great man.

They left the litter and entered a large shop. There Augustus bought many gifts for the young man—new arms, a beautiful corselet, a girdle of the look of knitted gold —for the Roman wore a girdle in Judea— articles of apparel suited to the climate of the Far East. The shop had filled with people, who tried to cover their curiosity by the purchase of trifles.

"This cloth would make a fine toga," said the shopkeeper.

The emperor surveyed it closely.

"Let me hold it up to the light and then you will see its texture," the other continued.

"You are a hard master," said Augustus. "You would have us walk on the housetops to show the fineness of our togas? It is enough. Let us pass, good people."

A cheer, starting at the shop door, went to the far sides of the city. It signified that the emperor was out among the people and in his best mood.

Their nomenclator cleared a way for them to the litter and they sat down again, facing each other, the emperor and the boy.

"If I had your riches," the great man remarked, as they went on, "I wonder what I should do with them."

"You jest with me, good father," said Vergilius.

"Nay, but I envy you; for have you not youth and love and the beauty of Apollo?"

He laid his hand upon the arm of the boy, and there was in his voice and manner a gentleness to make one regret that he lived not in a better time; for, perhaps, after all, he was what he had to be as the ruthless conqueror of a savage world.

"And I—what have I but burdens I dare not lay aside? When I sleep, even, they press upon me. I am weary — but if I should let them fall, what, think you, would happen?"

His keen eyes, seeing before them, possibly, the great down-rush to madness, pressed a glance into the very soul of the young man. The latter started to reply, but with a look the emperor forbade him.

"Think, good youth—learn to think. It will profit you—there is so little competition. By-and-by Rome will need you."

Gently, forcefully this teacher of statesmen had given the young knight his first lesson. It was nearing its end now. The

litter had stopped hard by the gate of
the Lady Lucia.

"I wonder how you knew my destina-
tion," said Vergilius.

"You credit me with small discernment.
Learn to know things that are not told you
—it is the beginning of wisdom."

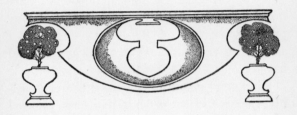

## Chapter 10

RRIA met them in the atrium. She saw not the great father of Rome, but only her lover, and ran to him with a little cry of delight.

The playful emperor mounted a chair and stood looking down at them.

"I am so small here in the presence of this great king," said he, as they turned to him. "Were my head as high as the ceiling I am sure I should not be seen."

"What king, good father?" said Arria, bowing low.

"Love! 'Tis better, I have heard, to be

ruler of one than of many. You give him kisses, little tyrant, and me not a glance."

He looked down, smiling at the pretty maiden.

"Because 'tis he I love," said she, her cheeks red with blushes, her eyes upon her sandals. "You—you have been cruel."

"I am sadly out of favor," said Augustus, playfully, stepping to the floor. "If the great king dared, I am sure he would cut off my head, now. Let him not condemn me without trial. Remember the law of Rome."

"You are sending my love away." Her voice trembled as she spoke.

"And happy are you, sweet girl, to have so much to give to your country."

There was a moment of silence. Then said the emperor: "Be merry. 'Tis not for long."

" 'Tis a thousand years!" said she, sadly.

He was fond of the young, and her frank innocence appealed to all best in the heart of the old emperor. He turned to greet the Lady Lucia.

113

"Come with me, son of Varro," said Arria, taking the arm of her lover and leading him away. "It will soon be to-morrow."

"And I am acquitted?" So spoke the emperor.

"You are condemned to the company of my mother," said Arria, quickly.

She wore a tunic of the color of violets, with not a jewel. Now she led her lover to a heap of yellow cushions in the triclinium.

"Dear Vergilius," said she, turning to him with a serious look as they sat down; "tell me again—say to me again how you love me." She held his hand against her cheek and her eyes looked into his.

"Oh, my beloved! I have thought of naught else since I saw you. I have heard your pretty feet and the rustle of your tunic in my dreams; I have felt the touch of your hands; every moment I have seen your face—now glowing with happiness, now white and lovely with sorrow. And, dear,

114

I love its sorrow—I confess to you that I love its sorrow better than its happiness. I saw in your sad eyes, then, a thing dearer than their beauty. It told me that you felt as I feel—that you would live and, if need be, die for the love of me."

The girl listened thoughtfully, and moved close to her lover; he took her in his arms. She had dreamed of many things to say, but now she only whispered to him, her lips against his ear, the simple message: "I love you, I love you, I love you." Then: "But I forgot," said she, pushing him away, a note of fear in her voice. She straightened the folds of her tunic, and drew the transparent silk close to her full, white bosom. It was all unconscious as the trick of a wooing bird.

"And what did you forget?" he inquired.

"That you are you, and a man," said she, sighing. "In some way it is—it is such a pity. I dare not suffer you to caress me. And yet—and yet, I do love it."

"And your lips," said he, embracing her, "they are to me as the gate of Elysium!"

"It may be we are now in the islands of the blest and know them not," she whispered.

She tried to draw herself away.

"I will not let you go. Indeed, I cannot let you go."

"And I am glad," she answered, with a little laugh, her hand caressing his brow. "I do love the feel of your arms and your lips—beautiful son of Varro!"

"I will not let you go until—until you have promised to be my bride. Think, the term is only two years."

"Be it one or many, I will be your bride," said she. "And although you were never to return, yet would I always wait for you and think of this day."

She drew herself away and sat thoughtful, her chin upon her hands.

"Now are you most beautiful," said he, "with that little touch of sorrow in your face. It gives me high thoughts to look at you."

While they were thus sitting a woman, well past middle age, came into their presence. She stopped near the feet of Arria. It was her grandmother, the Lady Claudia, once a beauty of the great capital, now gray and wrinkled, but still erect with patrician pride.

Vergilius had risen quickly, bowed low, and kissed her hand.

"I often saw you, son of my friend, when you were a child," said she. "I remember when you were young you went away with the legions."

"To learn the art of war," he answered.

"Sit down, dear grandmother," said the girl, as he brought a chair. "Now let her hear you tell me why it is that you have chosen me, dear Vergilius — let her hear you."

"I know not. Perhaps because your beauty, sweet girl, is like the snare of the fowler and brought me to your hand. Then something in your eyes captured the heart of me—something better than beauty. It is

117

the light of your soul. Love and peace and innocence and gentleness and all good are in it. That is why."

The two embraced each other. The Lady Claudia rose and came and put her hands upon them, and her voice trembled with emotion.

"They are beautiful," said she, "the kisses of the young, and their words are as the music of Apollo's lyre. I thank the gods I have seen it all again. But you are going away to-morrow. Son of Varro, be not as other men. Remember it is not well for women to live apart from the men they love."

"I leave at daybreak," said the young knight. " 'Tis for two years, so said the emperor; for 'only' two years."

"She shall not be as others I have known," said the Lady Claudia. "It is an evil time, good youth; but, remember, as men are so are women. Last night I dreamed a wonderful dream of you two, and of a sweet, immortal love between men

118

and women. Some say the dreams of men are, indeed, the plans of the gods. Pray to them. It may be they will give you this great love."

"It is here—it is in her soul and mine!" the youth declared, his arm about Arria. "It has prepared us for any trial—even parting."

"I have so much happiness already," said the girl. "So much — it will keep me through many years."

"Then it is the great love, and I thank the gods I have seen it," said the Lady Claudia. "Who may say where it shall end?" She came near them as she spoke and offered her cheek to the boy. He kissed her, and she went away with tears upon her face.

"Now you are brave and strong with this great love in you," said Vergilius. "Let it bear you up as I leave the palace. Promise you will not cry out. If you do, my beloved, I shall hear always the sound of mourning when I think of you."

"Then I shall not weep," said she,

bravely, but with a little quiver in her voice.

She knew the old story of a young man's love—how often he went away with sweet words, to return, if ever, hardened to stern trials and bloody work, his vows long forgotten.

"For your sake, dear Vergilius, I will be calm," she added.

"Now sit here," said he, as he led her to the heap of cushions, "just as I saw you a little time ago. Rest your chin upon your hands. There; now your soul is in your eyes. Let me see only this picture as I go."

He took a handful of her curls and let them fall upon her shoulders. Then he crowned her with a sprig of vervain from a vase near by.

"I will not weep—I will not weep," she repeated, her voice trembling as he touched her hair.

He moved backward slowly, as one might leave a queen. Her eyes followed him, and suddenly she rose and flew to his arms again.

"I will not weep—I will not weep," said she, brokenly. Again he held her to his breast.

"Though you get fame and glory, forget not love," she whispered.

"Dear one," he exclaimed, kissing her, "this hour shall be in every day of my life."

"But with adventures and battles and the praise of kings it is so easy to forget."

"But with one so noble and so beautiful at home it will be easy to remember. Let us be brave. I am only a woman myself to-day. Help me to be a man."

He led her again to the cushions, and she sat as before—a picture, now, beyond all art, sublime indeed with love and sorrow and trustfulness and repression. It was that look of abnegation upon her that he remembered.

"I shall not rise nor speak again, dear son of Varro," said she. "You shall know that my love for you has made me strong.  See, dear love.  Look at my face and see how brave I am."  Her voice, now calm, had in it some power that touched him deeply. It was the great, new love between men and women — forerunner of the mighty revolution.

He stood silent, looking down at her. The song of a nightingale rang in the great halls.  He turned and brought a lyre that lay on a table near them.  She took it in her hands.  Then it seemed as if her sorrow fell upon the strings, and in their music was the voice of her soul.

He bowed before her, whispering a prayer; he put all his soul into one long look and quickly went away.

Then she rose and ran to the end of the banquet-hall.  "I can hear his voice," she whispered.  "No, I must not go—I must not go."

A moment followed in which there came to her a sound of distant voices.  She stilled her sobs and listened.  She ran towards the

122

loved voice and checked her eager feet. She stood a moment with arms extended. The sound grew fainter and a hush fell. She ran to the white statue of the little god Eros, and, kneeling, threw her arms around the shapely form and wept bitterly.

## Chapter 11

HE dark was lifting as Vergilius entered the Field of Mars. There were lanterns about his litter, and far and near, in lines and clusters, he could see lights on the plain, some moving, some standing still. Hard by the Tiber he joined a small troop of horse, and vaulting on the shaft of his lance, mounted a white charger. Manius wheeled into place beside him at the head of the column. A quæstor called the roll.

"Ready?" Vergilius inquired, turning to Manius.

"All ready," the other answered.

Then a trumpet sounded and those many

feet had begun the long journey to Jerusalem. They made their way to the Forum.
Scores of women and children of the families
of those departing had gathered by the gold-
en mile - stone. The troop halted. Those
who had been waiting in the dank, chill air
sought to press in among the horses. It
was hard to keep them back. Vergilius,
full of his own sorrow, felt for them and
gave them good time. A little group, in
gray pænula and veils, were watching from
without the crowd. He moved aside, beckoning to them.

"Make your farewells," said he, as they
came near. "We shall be off in a moment."

A beautiful white hand was extended to
him. He took it in his, and then quickly
pressed it to his lips.

"Farewell, dear love!" he whispered.

A quick pressure answered him, and the
veiled figure turned away. Then a trumpet - call, a flash of blue vexilla and silver
eagles in the air, and, a moment later, some
eighty hoofs were drumming in the Appian

Way. For a little the horsemen heard them that were left behind, wailing.

"It is like a sticking of pigs to leave a lot of plebeian women," said Manius, when the sound was far out of hearing.

"An arrow in the heart of the soldier, but I think it good," said Vergilius. "For a time, at least, Rome will be dear to him."

There were forty men riding in the troop, all lancers, saving a few slingers and bowmen. They rattled over the hard Way at a pace of fifteen miles an hour. It was an immense, rock-paved road — this Appian Way—straight, wide, and level, flinging its arches over fen, river, and valley, and breaking through hill and mountain to the distant sea. No citizen might bring his horse upon it unless a diploma had been granted him—it was, indeed, for the larger purposes of the government. After two hours they drew up at a posting - house and changed horses. They rode this mount some forty miles, halting at a large inn, its doors flush with the road. A transport and postal train bound for Rome was expected shortly, and, before eating, Vergilius wrote a letter and had it ready when the wagons came rattling in a deep-worn rut, behind teams of horses moving at a swift gallop. There were five wagons in the train, bearing letters and light merchandise from the south. Hard by was one of the wheelwright-shops that lined the great thoroughfare. The train stopped only a moment for water and a new wheel, then rushed along on its way to the capital. A light meal of bread and porridge, half an hour of rest, and again, with new horses, the troop was in full career. A sense of loneliness grew in the heart of the youth as he journeyed. Lover and soldier had fought their duel, and the latter was outdone. But the lover's courage was now sorely tried. Every mounted courier hastening to Rome on the south road bore a letter from the young man to her he loved. He met a legion of infantry going north, and envied every soldier, sweating under a set pace of four miles to the hour and a burden of sixty pounds—shield, helmet, breast-plate, pilum, swords, intrenching tools, stakes for a palisade, and corn for seventeen days.

A trireme was waiting for them on the Adriatic Sea, and Vergilius, Manius, and their escort sailed to northwestern Macedonia, mounted horses again, galloping over the great highway to Athens; crossed by trireme to Ephesus, thence to Antioch by the long sea-road, and, agreeably with orders, they began to leave their men at forts along the frontier.

Events on the way filled him with contempt for his country and for himself. Here and there he met people travelling under imperial passes that gave them the use of the road and a right of free levy for subsistence, often much abused. These travellers were people of leisure from the large cities, wont to stretch their power to the point of robbery. He saw them seizing slaves and cattle from terrified agrarians; he saw Manius strike a man down for re-

128

senting insults to his daughter; he saw the deadly toil of the oarsmen, the bitter punishment of the cross.

His heart was now sore and sensitive. Was it the new love which had flung off its shield of sternness and left it exposed to every lash that flew? The misery of others afflicted him. Thoughts of injustice grew into motives of action, the loss of faith into the gain of unutterable longing. Who were these gods who heard not the cry of the weak and were ever on the side of the strong? Were they only in those hands of power that flung their levin from the Palatine? Could he, who had learned to love innocence and purity, love also the foul harpy which Rome had become? It seemed to him difficult to reconcile the love of Arria and the love of Rome. Was the time not, indeed, overdue when the wicked should tremble and the proud should bow themselves, according to that song of the slave-girl?

From Antioch they turned southward,

passing the cloistered plain paved with polished marble, and hurried to Damascus. Thence they rode to Jerusalem. The troop had dwindled to a squad of six, and came slowly into the ancient capital at dawn. From afar they could hear bugles at the castle of Antonia.

"They are changing the guard," Manius remarked.

Having entered the city gates, they passed throngs of cattle and their drivers and many worshippers hurrying to the temple. One of the latter stopped, and, pointing to the eagles and the medallion of Augustus on their signa, shouted loudly:

"I thank Thee, O God, and the God of my fathers, that I am not of them who provoke Thine anger with the graven image."

A chant of many voices from the temple roof floated over the plain, saying:

"The light has come as far as Hebron."

Vergilius turned, looking up at the splendid Doric temple of Jerusalem. As he looked, the sun's rays fell on a great, golden lantern before a thicket of high columns in its eastern portico. It was the signal for another outburst of trumpets.

"They are now making incense for the nostrils of Jehovah," said Manius. "Soon they will offer him one of the most beautiful lambs in Judea."

In a few moments they drew up at the castle of Antonia. News of their coming had reached Jerusalem by courier, three days before. The captain of the guard repeated part of the introduction.

"Vergilius, son of Varro, sent by the great father?" said he, in a tone of inquiry.

"And worn with much riding," said the young knight.

"I have a message for you. It is from the king."

"He would see me at once," said Vergilius, having read it.

"The sooner you go the more gracious you will be like to find him," said Manius, with a smile.

"My apparel! It is on the transport and has not yet arrived."

"But you have arrived, and forget not you are in the land of Herod—a most impatient king."

"He will not know, however, that we have come," Vergilius answered.

"Friend of Cæsar," said the captain of the guard, "within an hour he will know everything you have done since you entered the city—whither you went, to whom you spoke, and what you said, and perhaps even what you thought."

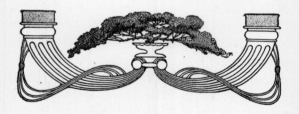

HE characters of Herod and Augustus were as far apart as their capitals. Extremes of temperament were in these two. The Roman was cold, calm, of unfailing prudence; the Jew hot-blooded, reckless, and warmed by a word into startling and frank ferocity. The one was keen and delicate, the other blunt and robust. The emperor was a fox, the king a lion. Herod and his people were now worried with mutual distrust. He had no faith in any man, and no man—not even the emperor by whose sufferance he held the crown—had any faith in him. The king feared the people and the people feared the king.

Herod began his career with good purposes. An erect, powerful, and handsome youth of Arabic and Idumæan blood, brave with lance and charger, he raided the bandit chieftain Hezekias and slew him, with all his followers. The Sanhedrim thought not of his valor but only of the ancient law he had broken. They put him on trial for usurping the power of life and death. In the midst of his peril he escaped, taking with him the seed of those dark revenges which, when he got the crown, destroyed all save a single member of the old court of justice and the confidence of his people.

His household became the scene of bloody intrigues which even stirred the tongue of Cæsar with contempt. Herod became the dupe of a designing sister, of base flatterers, and of an evil and ambitious son. They undermined his confidence in all who deserved it. His beloved wife Mariamne, his two sons Alexander and Aristobulus, and

134

many others of exceptional good repute in the kingdom were unjustly put to death. Then, swiftly, as he penetrated the maze of plot and counterplot, those who had fooled him began to fall before his wrath. He was now, indeed, a forlorn, loveless, and terrible creature.

Many thought him afflicted with madness. There were noble folk in Jerusalem who said they had seen the body of Mariamne embalmed in honey, above the king's chamber, where every day he could look upon it. Some had seen him wandering about the palace at night with a candle, mourning over his loss and raging at his own folly. Some had seen him so shaken by remorse that he roared like a lion goaded by hunger and the lance. At such a time it was, indeed, a peril to come before him. Plots against his life had worried him, and, distrusting his helpers, he was wont to go about the city in disguise seeking information. Twice he had forgiven Antipater, his favorite son, for crimes in the royal household.

135

Now, in his seventy-sixth year, the king was, indeed, sorely pressed with trouble. Jerusalem was the centre of a plot formidable and far-reaching. Its object was, in part, clear to him, or so he thought, and with some reason. It seemed to aim at his removal and the crowning of a mysterious king of prophecy, who, many said, was now waiting the death of Herod. It baffled him. He saw signs that many had their heads together in this plot. So far, however, he had not been able to lay hands upon them. There were many theories about the new king. They were strange and conflicting and zealously put forth. They differed as to whether he were yet born and as to his divinity, his character, and his purposes. The Sanhedrim held that when he came into the world there would be certain signs and portents seen of all men. This conflict of authority increased the confusion of Herod. When Vergilius came to his capital the king was mired on the very edge of the great mystery.

Powers of darkness ruled the city of Jerusalem. The sword, the lance, the dagger, and the wheel were wreaking vengeance and creating new perils while they were removing old ones. The king had tried vainly to repair the past. He gave freely to the poor; he erected gorgeous places of amusement; he built the new temple and a great palace in the upper city. The splendor of the latter structures had outdone the imperator. No shape born of barbaric dreams, to be slowly spread upon the earth in marble and gold, had so taxed the cunning and the patience of human hands. Such, in brief, were the character, the troubles, the home, and the city of Herod.

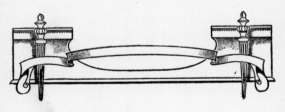

# Chapter

## 13

IN travel-worn garb Vergilius went early to see the king. Accustomed to the grandeur of Rome itself, he yet saw with astonishment the beautiful groves, the lakes, canals, and fountains sparkling in the sunlight which surrounded the great marble palace of Herod. In the shadow of its many towers, each thirty cubits high, Vergilius began to feel some dread of this terrible king. At least fifty paces from the door of his chamber, in the great hall abovestairs, he could hear the growl of the old lion. In Herod was the voice of wrath and revenge and terror. His words came rolling out in a deep, husky, guttural tone, or leaped forth hissing with anger. Some officials stood by the king's door with fear and dread upon their faces. A young woman of singular beauty was among them.

"O Salome, daughter of Herod," said one, "the king would have you come to-morrow. He is in ill humor with the plotters."

"And I with him," said she, stamping her foot.

An usher had presented Vergilius at the door. As Herod's daughter proudly turned away, she came face to face with the young Roman noble. For one moment their eyes held each other. A chamberlain approached Vergilius, whispered a few inquiries, and then led him before the king. Herod was having a bad day.

"Traitors!" he hissed. In a voice like the menacing growl of a savage beast he added: "May their eyes rot in their heads! Go! I have heard enough, bearer of evil tidings."

Far down the great chamber in which half a cohort could have stood comfortably, in a carved chair on a dais, under a vault and against a background of blue, Babylonian tapestry, sat the king. A priest had bowed low and was now leaving his presence. The chamberlain announced, in a loud voice, "Vergilius, son of Varro, of Rome, and officer of the fatherly and much-beloved Gaius Julius Cæsar Octavianus Augustus."

The king sat erect, a purple tarboosh and crown of wrought gold upon his head. As Vergilius approached, the dark, suspicious eyes of Herod were surveying him from under long, quivering tufts of gray hair. His great body, in its prime, must have been like that of Achilles.

"Stand where you are, son of Varro," said the king, as he moved nervously. His broad shoulders were beginning to bend a little under their burden of trouble and disease. The harrow of pain and passion had roughened his face with wrinkles. His manner was alert and watchful.

"Have you seen my son?" he inquired, quickly.

"Yes, great sire, and he was well."

"And is he not comely?"

"Ay, and brave with his lance."

"And a born king," said Herod. "I have fixed my heart upon him. I have no other to love—but the great imperator. And how is he?"

"I left him well, good sire."

"Stand a moment, son of Varro," said the king, with an impatient gesture. An attendant approached him and spoke in a low tone. Herod snarled like a huge cat when the lance threatens.

"Break him on the rack," he muttered; "and unless he tell, crucify him — crucify him. He shall do me no further injury. That priest Lugar, bring him back to me. Quickly now, bring him to me!"

The attendant hurried away, soon returning with him who had retired as Vergilius entered the king's chamber.

"Saw you the men of learning in Ascalon?" the king demanded.

"I did."

"What said they?"

There was a moment of silence.

"Out with it," said the king, fiercely. "Must I put every man upon the rack? Speak, and that you may tell the truth I shall not demand their names."

"They, also, look for the new king," said Lugar. "Many believe he is already born. They say that on your death he will declare himself."

"And they, too, pray for my death?"

"Most earnestly, my beloved king."

"Traitors!" said Herod, and as he spoke his powerful hands were tearing his kerchief into rags. "I shall soon change the burden of their prayers. Go tell them this: the day I die two of the wisest men from every city in the kingdom shall die also. Go everywhere, and tell these learned doctors they had best pray for my good health."

The priest bowed before his king and
retired. The pagan noble looked up at
this ruler of the land of the one God and
felt a thrill of horror. Herod, turning
quickly, beckoned to the young knight, his
wrinkles quivering with anger. Now, indeed, he was like a lion at bay.

"Ha-a!" he roared, and his head bent
slowly and his voice fell to a low rumble as
he continued. " 'Tis an evil time in Jerusalem. I weary of this long fight with
traitors. They grind their points; they
stir poison; they swarm in the streets.
They rob me of my friends, and now—now
they seek alliance with Jehovah to rob me
of my throne. 'Tis well you should know
and beware. I have a plan which will make
them desire my good health. Report to
Quirinus, and remember"—he took a hand
of the youth in both of his with a fawning
movement—"I have need of friends."

That very day an order went forth that
certain of the learned men of every city be
assembled in the amphitheatre at Jericho,

and be there confined to wait the further pleasure of the king. It was a bold plan through which Herod hoped to confound his enemies and insure his safety. He decreed that on the day of his death all these men should be executed.

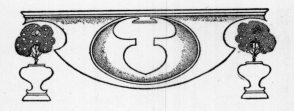

## Chapter
### 14

MONG the orderlies at the castle was one David, a young Jew, whose face and bearing had attracted the eye of Vergilius. There was in both something admirable and familiar. Straightway the tribune chose the young Jew for his own service, and soon held him in high esteem. Together they set out one morning, with a troop of horse, bound for the southern limit of Samaria. Thus quickly orders had arrived from the emperor. They sent Vergilius on a journey to inspect roads and report "as to hopes, plans, and theories of import to the king."

That morning as they left the old city, Vergilius and the young Jew rode abreast.

"Tell me," said the former, presently, "what know you of the new king?"

"Of him I have thought much and know little," said David. "My mother taught me to look for him. That was before the evil days."

"And you learned what of her?"

"Little save the long hope. She taught me an old chant of the coming. If you wish, I will sing it."

Being bidden, he sang, as she had sung who hushed the revels of Antipater, of signs and fears and of arrows to fly as the lightning. Words, melody, emotion, the note of inveterate wrong, were those of the slave-girl.

"The same nose and blue eyes, and fair, curly locks—the same feeling and chant of faith," said Vergilius, thoughtfully. "Did you not live in Galilee and suffer ill fortune?"

"We lived in Galilee, and, by-and-by, were as those hurled into Gehenna."

146

"And have you a sister in Rome?"

"I have a sister, but know not where she may be. Cyran the Beloved, so my mother called her."

Then Vergilius told his companion how he had won her from the son of Herod and left her in the keeping of Arria. David wept as he listened.

When the tale was finished he spoke bitterly: "'Twas she — the Beloved. My father was put to death, his property seized, his wife and children dragged to captivity. My heart is faint with sorrow. God! I weary of thy slowness.

"Send, quickly send the new king, whose arrows
    shall fly as the lightning,
Making the mighty afraid and the proud to bow
    low and the wicked to tremble."

For a moment they rode in silence. David was first to speak.

"Forgive me," said he, with fear of his imprudence. "My tongue has gone too far. I am true to Herod, being his debtor, for he gave me freedom. But I am of the house of David."

"Fear not," said Vergilius. "Never shall I betray the broken hearted. I give you friendship."

"And I give you gratitude," was the answer of the Jew.

"I am as a child here in Judea and seek understanding. You shall be my teacher."

For a time neither spoke ; soon David asked: "Will you tell me of her my sister is now serving?"

"Of all the daughters of Rome she is noblest. We love each other. Ah, friend! 'Tis a wonder—this great love. My tongue halts when I think of it."

He paused, in meditation.

"I have heard much of it here in Judea— a love that exalts the soul," said David.

"And changes the heart of man with all that is in it. My love has filled me with a tender feeling for all women; it has made me to hate injustice and even to complain of the gods."

"To complain of the gods!" said David, turning and looking into the face of his friend.

"It does seem to me they set a bad example and are too childish for the work they have to do, but still—still I bow before them."

"I do not understand you," said David.

"They are given to spite, anger, vanity, lust, revenge, and idleness. Cæsar is greater than they. He has learned self‑control. And this new king of your faith, who, you tell me, is to conquer the world—he is no better."

"And why think you so?"

"He is to conquer the world. Good sir, it has been conquered—how many times! He shall make the mighty afraid—have they not often trembled with fear and perished by the sword? He shall fling arrows of just revenge, as if our old earth were not already soaked in the blood of the wicked. Ah, my David, I wonder not you long for a king of the sword and the arrow. Revenge is ever the dream of the oppressed. But I have dreamed of a greater king."

"Tell me who?"

"He would be like this love in me," said Vergilius. "If it were to go abroad— if it were only to find the hearts of the mighty—what, think you, would happen?"

"Ay, if it were to go from friend to friend and from neighbor to neighbor," said the young Jew, "it would indeed conquer the world."

"And there would be neither war nor injustice."

"Tell me," said David. "Are there many lovers like you in Rome?"

"Some half a score that I have heard of, and I doubt not there be many."

"'Tis the candle of the Lord—the preparation of the heart of man," said David. "I do believe his arrow shall be that of love."

"This feeling in me has kindled a great desire," said Vergilius. "I burn for knowledge."

Then said the young Jew: "Let us find my kinsman, Zacharias—a priest of holy life and great learning. Through his aged wife a miracle has been accomplished. I learn that she has given birth, and many have journeyed far to see the child. There be some who say that he is, indeed, the king of promise, albeit I have no such opinion."

"Why?"

"There shall be signs in the deep of the heavens, and we have not seen them."

"Where may we find the priest?"

"In the village of Ain Karim, yonder."

They could see its low dwellings and the dome of its synagogue. The Roman halted near the abode of Zacharias, while David took their followers to the inn. Suddenly the young Roman saw an aged priest approaching with a child in his arms.

"I have a message for you," said the man of God, stopping near the Roman officer.

"And I seek it," said Vergilius, looking at the long, gray beard of the venerable priest.

151

"It is borne in upon me to say to you that the kingdom of heaven is at hand."

"Tell me of the king," said Vergilius. "I do thirst for knowledge."

"He shall be the prince of peace."

Vergilius looked thoughtfully at the old priest, who now sat down as if weary.

"And he shall conquer with the sword?"

"Nay, but as it is written, 'he shall judge among the nations and shall rebuke many people; and they shall beat their swords into ploughshares and their spears into pruning-hooks; nation shall not lift up sword against nation, neither shall they learn war any more.'"

Now the Roman was alert to hear. His ideal, which had taken form at the altar of peace and grown with his love, was being set up before him.

"But the nations are stubborn," said he. "Tell me, O wise and learned man, how shall he subdue them?"

"By the love of God, almighty and everlasting."

"God, almighty and everlasting," said Vergilius. "I know him not."

"I do but defile myself to speak with you, worshipper of idols," sternly spake the priest. "And yet I am constrained to instruct you. Listen — there is a power which even Rome has not been able to conquer. Know you what power it is?"

The young tribune was recounting the peoples of the earth, when Zacharias continued:

"'Tis the God of the Jews. Rome has conquered his people, but mark how he stands. And what is there of wrong that his law cannot remedy? Tell me, is there no injustice in your land?"

"There is much," said the young Roman.

"And so I know—but name it."

"Well, for one thing, men torture and kill their slaves."

"And in the law of the one God 'tis written, 'Thou shalt not kill.'"

After a thoughtful moment Vergilius added: "And the strong prey upon the weak, seizing their property and holding it for their own."

"And the one God commands, 'Thou shalt not steal'; and again, 'Thou shalt not covet thy neighbor's house, thou shalt not covet thy neighbor's wife, nor his man-servant, nor his maid-servant, nor his ox, nor his ass, nor anything that is thy neighbor's.'"

"But you have injustice, also, in Judea."

"Ay, because there be evil men who obey not the law of God. But presently they shall be put to shame. Here is he that is come to prepare the way of the Lord."

The child was now asleep, his head on his father's knee.

"John," said the priest, tenderly looking down.

But the little one continued to sleep, and a wonderful peace and beauty had come upon him.

"And this new king — whence shall he come and how shall we know him?" the young Roman persisted.

"Conceived of God, he is now in the womb of his mother," said the priest. "Soon—very soon, he shall enter the gate of the world. The ground is ready and he shall be like a sower, and his seed shall be love, and peace shall be his harvest. If ye would know him, behold this face."

He touched the brow of the child. "Son of darkness," he continued, "look upon the son of light! The faith of Mizraim or the wisdom of Hillel could show you no more. Do you see the new light shining within this lovely veil of flesh? Look, and you shall know the fashion of his countenance, and that his hand shall make no wound."

The priest rose, and, lifting the child in his arms, went away, saying, "His peace be with you."

The young Roman stood looking at the sweet face that lay on the shoulder of him departing. The great hope of Judea had entered his heart — the hope of a just king to rule the nations and point the way to eternal life.

155

On his return he bought a statue representing a beautiful young boy. He set it up in his chamber, and, kneeling, prayed to it as the one God who forbade killing and theft and every evil practice of men. He prayed for understanding; he prayed, also, that he might see her he loved. But this new God seemed as deaf to his entreaty as had been those of the pagan temples. Groping for light, he turned to the young David. Then first he learned that God, being jealous, hated the image of everything that has the breath of life. His understanding had diminished, for, in this matter, the one God was like the many. He questioned the Jew. "Wonder not," said his friend, "that God hates the symbol of ancient error. It has been as a cloud upon the sun."

Vergilius had taken a palace and filled it with treasures, for, possibly, he had thought, some day she would see all. Now its noble statues were sent away—a kind of sacrifice to the God of the Jews. But

156

there was one he could not part with—a copy of the lovely Venus of Alcamenes which his mother had sent to him. He concealed her in a closet, contenting himself with a furtive glance at her now and then. He set up in his fancy a giant of benevolent face, and humbly sought his favor. Still he had no success.

Lying at table one night with Manius and Ben Joreb, he sought counsel of the latter.

"He that hath his prayer hath prayed wisely," said the priest. "You have much to learn."

"How, and of whom?" said Vergilius.

"There is in Jerusalem a council of learned men. They expound the Scripture and study all mysteries of the faith."

"And who are they?"

"I would I knew. Being wise, they are unknown."

"Unknown!"

"So I have heard. They have knowledge of him who is to come, and Herod is very jealous."

"True," said Vergilius.   "I would I were of them who know."

"If it may be so you shall have word to-morrow," said the priest.

Promptly Manius relieved the tension of curiosity.

"Vergilius, I drink to you — the new commander of the cohorts," said he, rising.

"I reserve my thanks for more information," said Vergilius.

"It will come," said Manius, who then left with the priest in his company.

Soon the former added, in a low tone: "He may be of some value before he dies."

"Ah, yes, but he will die young," said the other.

# Chapter

## 15

EXT day among his letters were two of value in the history of Vergilius — one from the procurator, apprising him of his appointment to command the cohorts, the other a communication with no signature, the source of which was, in his view, quite apparent. This latter one gave him the greater satisfaction. It conveyed, in formal script, the following message:

"To One Seeking Wisdom in Prayer

"If you would share in the deliberations of the Council of the Covenant, be at the well of Nicanor, which is opposite the tenth column in

the king's portico of the temple, at the second
sounding of the sacred horns on the Day of Atonement. There wait until one shall come and ask
what you are seeking, and you shall answer,
'Knowledge of the one God.' Then, if he turns
away, follow him and do as he bids you."

His opportunity had come. He waited
with the curiosity of a child. Soon, possibly, he should see the face of the great
Lawgiver and learn of things beyond the
valley of death. If all went well he would
amaze the people of Rome with wonder
stories and give them assurance of immortal life.

The city had been thronged with pilgrims
that day of the ancient festival. It was
turning dusk when Vergilius made his way
through crowded streets to the well of
Nicanor. Suddenly he heard a trumpet
signal, and then followed that moment of
silence when every tongue and foot and
wheel stopped, quickly, and all stood listening for the awful name spoken but once a
year.

Presently the shout of the high priest

rang like a trumpet - peal above the roofs
of the city. Then Jerusalem was all be-
girt and overflooded with song. Maidens,
white robed, were singing in distant vine-
yards; people were singing in the streets;
trained devotees were whirling and dancing
and chanting psalms in the court of the
Temple, while priest and Levite followed,
blowing, with all their power of lung, upon
the sacred horns.

In the midst of this outbreak a stranger
approached Vergilius at the well, saying,
"What seek you?" The young Roman
gave his answer, but was unable to see the
face of him who questioned. The stranger
turned away and bade him follow. Without more ceremony Vergilius walked behind him through narrow streets, wholly
unfamiliar, and presently descending a
stairway, came into a dark passage. They
halted, after a few paces, whereupon a loud
rap startled the new-comer. Soon he could
hear a door open. The stranger, taking his
hand, led him into some dark place. It

was all very strange, and like tales long
familiar, relating to the city of mysteries.
Standing there in the dark and silence, he
had some misgivings which gave way when
a voice addressed him as follows:

"You are now in the council-chamber of
the Covenant. We meet in darkness, so
that no shape or form or image may turn
our thought from the contemplation of him
who is most high and who hath his dwell-
ing in black darkness. Moreover, those
who are not seen shall have neither vanity
nor the will to deceive. Would you share
in our deliberations?"

Vergilius answered yes, and one of the
council then took his hand and adminis-
tered the oath of secrecy, and led him to
what seemed to be a large divan, where he
sat, shoulder to shoulder, between other
members of the council. He listened long
to the casuistry of learned men touching
prayer, atonement, and sacrifice. It led at
last to some discussion of the new king.

"Is there one here can tell me where and

when he shall be born?" was the query of Vergilius.

"We believe the Messiah is already born," said a councillor. "Moreover, some here have beheld his face."

"And where, then, does he dwell?" Vergilius inquired.

"That you shall know some day. At the next meeting of the council it may be told. We wait only for the fulness of time. He dwells in a distant city, and not long ago I spoke with him. He sent his love and greeting to every member of our council. He bids you wait his time, when all your prayers shall be answered."

"Shall there be signs of his coming?" So spoke Vergilius.

"There shall be signs, and you shall hear of them in this chamber."

"And what shall be the aim of the king?"

"To establish the reign of justice."

Vergilius queried much regarding the government of the new king, and got replies adding more to his curiosity than to his knowledge.

It was near the middle hour of the night when a voice announced: "The keeper of the new door will now leave the council."

Vergilius heard a stir coming near him in the darkness. Hands were laid upon him, and, presently, one took his arm and led him away. The two climbed a long flight of stairs and made hastily across a broad roof. At a railed opening they came to other stairs, and, descending, entered a passage, dark as had been the chamber. At its end the Roman received a password. Then a door swung and again he was on the pavements of Jerusalem, and, far away, could see the lights of Temple Hill.

His conductor, returning, announced the departure of "the new voice."

"We will now hear from the keeper of records," said one.

A voice quickly answered: "He secured a lock of his hair."

"And what says the keeper of the hidden light?"

Then said another voice: "He now sees but one obstacle."

"And what says the Angel of Death?"

A low, deep tone broke the silence in which all waited. "The sixth day before the kalends, he shall claim his own," so it answered.

"Enough," said the questioner. "The ways lead to safety. I bid you go."

One by one the councillors began to leave. There was no treading upon heels, for one was well out of the way before another was allowed to go. So cunningly was their room devised that half the exits led to one thoroughfare and half to another; and so many were they, it was said, no more than two councillors came or went by the same door. And of all who came, so say the records, not one knew another to be sure of him.

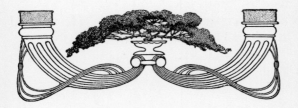

# Chapter 16

OR the king there were three great perils: the people, Cæsar, and his own family. The descendant of old John Hyrcanus of Idumæa — a Jew only by compulsion — had no understanding of the children of Moses. He tripped every day on the barriers of ancient law, and often his generosity was taken for defiance. Cæsar was not so hard to please. He had vanity and laws not wholly inflexible. Herod's family, with its evil sister, its profligate sons, its voluptuous daughters, its wives, of whom it is enough to say they were nine,

its intrigues and jealousies, gave him
greater trouble than either the kingdom
or the emperor. He built a city near
Jerusalem, on the sea. Magnificent in
marble and gold, Cæsarea stood for a
monument of Herodian troubles. Therein
he sought to amuse the people, to pacify
his kindred, and to flatter Cæsar. Its vast
breakwater; its great arches through which
the sea came gently in all weather; its
mosaic pavements washed daily by the salt
tide; its palaces of white marble; its great,
glowing amphitheatre—these were unique
in their barbaric splendor, albeit, in the
view of the people, an offence to God.

Among those who dwelt in Cæsarea was
Elpis, eighth wife of the king, with her
daughter Salome, whose praises had been
sung at the banquet of Antipater. Both
were renowned for beauty and the splendor
of their dress. Salome had the colors of the
far north, and that perfect and voluptuous
contour found only in marble figures of
Venus, above the great purple sea, and,

below it, in the daughters of men. She was tall, shapely, full blooded. They called her Salome, child of the sun, because she had the dark of night in her large eyes, the tints of morning in her cheeks, and the gold of noonday in her hair.

When Manius came to seek her hand the king said, with a smile: "My noble youth, she is for the like of Achilles—a man of heroic heart and size. Have you no fear of her?"

Quickly Manius replied: "Know you not, O king! my fathers fought with Achilles?"

"But they had the protection of the gods," said Herod, with a smile. "However, you may find her favor sufficient. I have heard her speak fair of you."

Now a quarrel had arisen between Elpis and a sister of Herod. So, therefore, to calm a tempest, the adroit king had sent his eighth wife to live by the sea.

It was a day near the nones of October, when the tribune went to Cæsarea with Manius. There in a great palace, erected by

the king, they met the two renowned women.
It was a fête day and the gay people of
Herod's court were in attendance.   Salome
was dancing, tabret in hand, her form showing through a robe of transparent silk as the
two entered.   Once before, at the door of
the king, Vergilius had seen her.

"See the taper of arm and leg," said
he, addressing his companion.   "She is
wonderful!"

A lithe and beautiful creature, she swayed
and bent, with arms extended, her feet,
now slow as the pinions of a sailing hawk,
now swift as the wings of a tilting sparrow.
She stopped suddenly, her form proudly
erect, looking at her lover.   Now she had
the dignity of a wild deer in the barrens.
With one hand she felt her jewelled hair,
with the other she beckoned to him.   The
young men approached her.

"Children of Æneas, I give you wel-
come," said she.   Then turning to Vergilius: "Did Manius tell you that I bade
him bring you here?"

"I knew not I was so honored."

"He is jealous. He will not permit me to embrace my little page. I have wished to meet you, noble tribune, ever since I saw you in my father's palace."

Her eyes were playful, as if they would try the heart of her lover.

"And when I saw you," said Vergilius, "I—I knew you were the betrothed of the assessor."

"And why?" she besought, with a smile.

"Because I heard him say in Rome that, of all the daughters of Judea, you were most beautiful."

Her eyes looked full upon his and he saw in them a glint of that fire which had begun to burn within her. He said to himself, as he came away, "Here is another Cleopatra —a woman made to pull down the mighty."

Next day from the daughter of Herod came a letter to the young tribune:

"NOBLE SON OF VARRO,—I have much to say concerning your welfare, and I doubt not you will desire to hear it. If I judge you rightly, come to the palace of my mother the second evening before the nones. An hour after sunset I will meet you at the gate of bronze. Say naught to Manius of your coming or of this letter."

"Temptress!" said he, crushing the sheet of scented vellum. "But she is beautiful," he added, wistfully. "She is like the Venus of Alcamenes. I would love well to look upon her again."

He smoothed out the crumpled vellum.

"'Say naught to Manius,'" he read again. "I like it not. I shall write to her that I have other business."

And so did he, although in phrases of regret, as became one addressing a daughter of the great king.

Sorely vexed, she thought ever of the noble beauty of the Roman youth, and became more eager to gain her purpose. It may be the girl bore for him a better feeling than she had ever known. She wished, if possible, to win him, knowing that her father would not be slow to help him

171

forward. The handsome youth had pleased her eye and might, also, gratify her ambition. Those days the art of intrigue was the study of a king's daughter; so, straightway, she invented a cunning plan. Knowing the great desire of Vergilius, she bribed the priest Lugar to give him crafty counsel. On the very morning of that second day the priest came to him.

"How fares your soul, noble tribune?" said Lugar.

"I feel it strong in me," said Vergilius.

"And you would know if it be strong unto salvation?"

"That would I gladly know."

"Come with me this night and you shall see your soul in the balance."

"And whither shall we go?"

"To the palace of Laban, steward of the king. I shall come for you soon after the ninth hour."

"And thereby increase my debt to you," said Vergilius. "Remember my soul may not be rejected for lack of gratitude."

Now in that hour which follows the beginning of night, Lugar and Vergilius were come to the place appointed. Slaves led them through a great hall to the banquet-chamber. There were the daughters of Laban, reclining in graceful ease. The banquet-table had been removed. Now they were taking their feast of old tales and new gossip. They rose and came to meet the young men. Tunics of jewelled gauze covered without concealing forms lovely as the sculptures of immortal Greece and redolent of all rare perfumes.

"And you would see a maidens' frolic?" said one to Vergilius.

Then said he: "Maidens are ever a delight to me."

"Ay, they make you to forget," said the girl.

He thought a moment before answering. "It may be true," said he. "But they keep you in mind of the power of woman."

Strains of the lyre broke in upon them. Suddenly the centre of the great room was

thronged with maidens. The young tribune
was full of wonder, knowing not whence
they had come. There was a wreath of
roses on each brow, and as they gathered
in even rank with varicolored robes upon
them, they reminded the knight of garden
walls in Velitræ. Quickly they began to
mingle, with feet tripping lightly, with
bodies bending to display their charms.
Threadlike, wavering gleams of ruby, pearl,
and sapphire seemed to weave a net
upon them. Such a scene appealed to the
love of beauty in Vergilius. It awoke dying but delightful memories of the pagan
capital—splendors of form and color, glowing eyes and pretty frolic.

"O Venus, mother of love!" he whispered, turning to admire a statue in the
dim - lit corner where he stood. Now the
eyes of Venus were covered with an arm.
Out went his hand to feel the shapely marble. It was warm, and slowly Venus began
to move, as did the strains of music, and,
presently, whirled away.

"How beautiful!" he said. "'Tis the magic of a dream."

His eyes were upon the form of Venus, taller than the others and more nobly fashioned.

"'Tis the great goddess come to earth," said he, turning to Lugar.

The music had ceased. The maidens, save two, had flung themselves upon rugs and couches. Venus and another were approaching the Roman.

"Daughter of Herod," said he, going to meet her, "I knew you not."

She took his arm and led him to one of the couches.

"You are very stubborn," said she, looking into his eyes. "You had 'business.'"

"So have I. We came here, as I thought, to confer with—with wise men."

"And not with wise women?"

"It may be. I had not learned to look for wisdom where there is beauty."

"And have I not wisdom? Ah, son of

Varro, my mother has taught me many
mysteries. I can read the future and the
past."

She leaned close to his ear and whispered,
her arm against his: "I believe in the
power of fate. I had much to say and you
had not the will to listen. It has brought
you and me together."

"To enchant me with your beauty?" he
inquired.

"Nay," said she, her cheek touching his
shoulder. "But to instruct you with my
wisdom. I see much in your face."

"And what see you?"

"Apollo!" she whispered, with a sigh;
"and the power to be great."

It flattered him, but he knew the sound
of fair words.

"In Rome," said he, laughing, "we be-
little with compliments."

"In Jerusalem we fill them with sincerity,
and often—"

He listened as the daughter of Herod
drew closer.

176

"They convey our love," she added, in a whisper.

"I learn wonderful things every day. But why think you I am to be great?"

"I know the mysteries of fate," she answered, quickly, and with a little resentment of his coldness. "But there is one thing in your way."

"And what?"

"Your work is to be in Judea, and you love, or think you love, a Roman maiden."

"I know that I love her," said he, quickly.

"But love is a great deceiver. You shall not take her for your wife."

"Why?" he demanded, turning and looking into the face of Salome.

Her dark eyes were now gazing into his, her hand softly stroking his bare arm.

"Because," she whispered, and now he could feel the motion of her shapely red lips upon his ear, "here, in Judea, you shall find one who loves you with a greater love."

His pulses were quick with passion. He

177

rose, turning from the daughter of Herod.
To his amazement the others had all departed. He and this living Venus of Judea
were alone.

She rose and spoke rapidly, her heart's
fire in her words! "Here the love of wom-
en is longer than their lives—greater than
their prudence or their hope of heaven."

She stood erect before him, her beauty
striving with the ardor of her words.

He looked down at her with a kind of fear
in his eyes.

She took his hand in hers. "My father
is fond of you," she continued. "Shall I
tell your future?"

"And I knew it for a moment hence I
should know all," he answered, covering
his eyes. She came near, and, caressingly,
put an arm about his neck. He could hear
a nightingale singing somewhere in the
great palace. It seemed to fling open the
gates of memory. He thought of his love
—sacred now above all things. His fear
of it was like as the fear of the gods had

been to his fathers. For a moment honor, wisdom, and love trembled in the balance. Suddenly he stood erect and put his hand upon the shoulder of Salome and gently pushed her aside.

He turned away, his left arm covering his eyes and his right moving in a gesture of protest. He staggered as one drunk with wine. Slowly he crossed the chamber, struggling to defend his soul.

"I dare not look upon your face again," said he, sternly.

She ran before and tried to stop him. "Hear me, son of Varro," said she. "It is my will to help you."

"I will not look upon your face again," he repeated.

She struck at his hand fiercely, her foot stamping on the floor. Now was she of the catlike tribe of Herod.

"Go, stupid fool!" The words came hissing from her lips. "I hate you!" She ran away, with impassioned laughter. He passed the door.

179

"To the evil honor is ever stupid," he said, to himself, as he left the palace. By-and-by he added, thoughtfully, "'Tis a mighty friend—this great love in me."

And said David, who was waiting when he returned: "They kept you long, my master."

"Yes; I have been fighting!"

"Fighting?"

"For the prize of heaven in the amphitheatre of hell. My love was my shield, the power of God my weapon."

"Friend, what mean you?"

"That an evil woman has tried to put the leash of fate upon me."

"How fared the battle?"

"It was my victory," said Vergilius; "and I do feel a mighty peace in me."

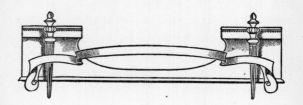

ERGILIUS had thought wisely of his temptation. Fate rules them only who are too weak to rule themselves, and the great leash of fate is the power of evil women. It was now to hasten the current of history in the old capital.

Salome sat with Manius in the great picture-room of her mother's palace. Guests had left the banquet-hall and gone to their homes. It was near the middle hour of the night and Herod's daughter was alone with the young assessor of Augustus.

"You shall choose," said she, "between

181

the daughter and the son of Herod. My
brother hates me, and I fear him. When he
is king, what, think you, would happen to
the husband of Salome, and what to her?
I should have to train my tongue to praise
him and my knees to bend. I should
need to bow my head for fear of losing it.
Know you not of Alexander and Aristobulus and the dear, beloved Mariamne—
how they died? You — poor fool! — you
would be lucky if he made you master of
the stables!"

"But he has promised—"

"Promised! If you care to live a day
after he is king remind him not of his
promises."

"Think you Antipater would dare to take
my life? I am an officer of Augustus."

"Oh, beautiful boy!" she laughed. "He
would be no toy of Cæsar. He dreams of
conquest. He will gather an army in Judea,
Parthia, and Arabia. He will attack Cæsar,
and Cæsar is growing old. Do you not
know it is long since Actium?"

Alarm had risen to the eyes of the young
Roman, his lips were now trembling.
"What is your plan?" he whispered.

"Betray the council," said she. "Tell
the king and write to Cæsar about it. So
you will prove your faithfulness and devotion. Loving Cæsar, you have been a spy
self-appointed. Antipater shall be put to
death, and we—we shall have honor and
glory and, maybe, a palace of many
towers."

She put her arms about his neck and gave
him a look whose meaning he understood.

"By all the gods! you are worthy to be
the wife as well as the daughter of a king,"
he whispered, his cheeks red with en-
thusiasm. "But they will think me a poor
spy if I give not the names of the conspirators, and how may I?"

"But the God-fearing fool, Vergilius—
you know he is of them?"

"I am sure—I heard his voice, but I have
not seen him."

"You shall see him," said she, with

rising fury in her eyes; "and I shall see
him"— she paused, her hands clinched,
her tongue sorting hot words—"melting in
fire," she added, fiercely. She clapped her
hands; she leaned forward, her body shak-
ing with a silent, horrible laughter of the
spirit.

A moment she seemed to dwell upon the
awful picture. Then, turning to Manius:
"Give the password to my father and let
him go and listen. I promise you their
names shall not be long a secret. He must
hear all. Give him plans of that chamber
so he may guard the exits."

"I will do my part, dear and wonderful
daughter of Herod! To - morrow I shall
begin the good work." So saying the
Roman embraced Salome and spoke his
farewell.

Having left her, he went to his own
palace and sat awhile pondering.

"But if Herod is there," said he to himself, "and the soldiers come in with lights
and the council members see me, they will

184

learn that I have betrayed them. And some may be there who know of my part in other enterprises. By showing proof— Jupiter! they would bring confusion or death upon me. I must not be there, and yet—and yet I must. They wait for the shrill voice to declare the fulness of time. Unless I be there the king may be no wiser for his coming. I will go, but I will not tell Herod of the long way underground to the street of tombs. I will announce the fulness of time and quit the council before its proclamation is made. Then the old lion may spring his trap, and who, save Ben Joreb, will know that I ever sat with traitors. And as for the priest, I shall warn him. I know that he is weary of Antipater and will take a share in the new enterprise."

13

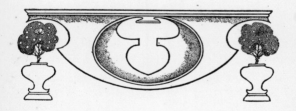

T was the day before the nones of November in Rome. The emperor had returned to his palace after opening the Ludi Plebeii. The people had hailed him as father, forgiver, peace-maker. A softened spirit, sweeping over the world, was come upon them. That day they had put in his hands a petition for new laws to limit the power of men over slaves. But in that matter he was bound to ancient custom by fetters of his own making. Once— he was then emperor of Rome but not of his own spirit—he had punished a slave by crucifixion for killing a pet quail. For that

186

act, one cannot help thinking, he must have
been harassed with regret. The sting of
it tempered his elation that November day.
He was, however, pleased with the spirit of
the people and his heart was full of sympathy and good-will.

On his table were letters from the south.
He lay comfortably in his great chair and
began to read them. Presently his body
straightened, the wrinkles deepened in his
brow. Soon he flung the letter he had been
reading upon his table and leaned back,
laughing quietly as he remarked to himself:

"Innocent, beautiful son of Varro! He is
making progress."

An attendant came near.

"Find my young Appius at once and
bring him to me," said the emperor, as he
went on reading his letters.

Appius, quickly found, came with all
haste to the great father of Rome.

"I have news for you," said the latter,
quietly, with a glance at his young friend.
He continued to read his letters.

"News!" said Appius.

"'Tis of Vergilius — the apt and youthful Vergilius. How swift, industrious, and capable is he! How versatile! How varied his attainments!"

"I am delighted."

The emperor turned his keen eyes on the young man, with a smile of amusement. Then he spoke, gently:

"'Tis only four months, and he has become a conspirator, and also a prophet, and is likely soon to be—what is that word they use in Judea?—an angel. You will start for Jerusalem to - morrow, my good Appius. And when you arrive there convey to him my congratulations."

"Your congratulations!"

"That he is upon earth to receive them," said the great man. He resumed his letters and continued speaking, slowly: "Tell him I have been asked to consider whether he should keep his head upon his shoulders, and that I have decided to refer the question to him. It will not come back to me.

Say, also, that he should have more light upon his friends, and that I have withdrawn my consent to his marriage."

The young man rose, a look of astonishment in his face.

"But shall I be in time?" said he, with some excitement.

"Learn composure, my good Appius. Herod may not be extremely polite to him, but—but he will wait."

That odd man, Gaius Julius Cæsar Octavianus Augustus, laughed silently as the youth was leaving. He beckoned to a slave, who halted Appius and turned him back.

"An escort will be on the campus at dawn," said the emperor. "I wish you a pleasant journey and will write you when to return."

Now there had been no changes of moment in the palace of the Lady Lucia, save one. The slave-girl, Cyran, had brought to Arria the inspiration of a new faith. The sister of Appius had begun to try it in secret prayers. Her mother had fallen ill of a

189

deadly fever so that none had hope of her
recovery, and the girl had prayed, and, lo!
her prayer had been answered. Letters from
Vergilius, full of the new light in him, had
confirmed her faith. And Arria confided
to her family and intimates knowledge of
her devotion to the one God. Soon the
religion of Judea had become a topic of
patrician Rome.

When Vergilius had left the capital, Antipater came every day for a time to the
palace of the Lady Lucia, and brought with
him many beautiful gifts. But Arria refused to see him or to accept the gifts he
had brought. Now the stubborn prince
had faith that when he was made king she
would no longer be able to resist him. If
he failed with splendor, he was beginning
to consider what he might do with power.

That day of the interview between
youth and emperor a letter came to Arria
from her lover. It began as follows:

"DEAR LOVE,—It has been a day illumined
with new honor and the praises of a king. Now,

before sleeping, I send these words to tell you that I have not forgotten. Every day I think of you, and my love grows. I see your face full of honor and the will to give all for me. Because it is in you, I love honor beyond all my hope of it, and—that look in your eyes—oh, it has made me to think gently and be kind! Now I tell you of a wonderful thing—this feeling is the very seed of friendship. The legate, the procurator, the high priest, and Herod himself, are my friends. I had only the will to serve, and now they insist that I shall command. After all, it is in no way remarkable—there be so few here who forget themselves for the good of the service. It all leads to a new and a great law—think of the good of others and you need have no thought of yourself. Consider this, my beloved, if every man loved a good woman as I love you a new peace would fill the world."

Then he told her of his discovery of David, the brother of Cyran, and their friendship.

## Chapter

### 19

WHEN Appius told his mother and his sister what Augustus had said to him, they were greatly distressed. But Arria would not believe that Vergilius had been guilty of dishonor. Such were her anxiety and her fear of injustice falling upon her lover, the girl would have it that she must go to Jerusalem with Appius. She would neither be turned away nor bear with dissuasion. Her brother told her not of the bitter message of Augustus, and, fearing the wiles of the Jewish prince, determined to take her with him. So, therefore, as the sun

rose on the nones of November in that
year of the birth of Jesus, they set out
with a troop of horse on the Appian Way.

They were midland in Thrace on their
way to Piræus, where a ship waited them,
when they were overtaken by the cavalcade
of Antipater. The prince, summoned by
Herod, was now returning, under royal
banners, to receive his inheritance of glory
and power. A letter had started him,
which, according to the great historian of
that time, was warm with affectionate
greeting. Antipater, also, was to take ship
for Judea. He had learned of the departure of Appius and Arria, and had pushed
his horses to the limit of their speed in
order to overtake them. When he first
saw the troop of the young Roman, he left
his column and came rushing on to greet
them.

The troop of Appius quickly faced about
and stood with raised lances.

"Proud son and daughter of Publius,"
said Antipater, drawing rein, "my heart,

my horses, and my men are at your service!"
He was now splendid in royal vestments
of purple and gold.

"Our gratitude is not less than our surprise," said Appius. "How came you flying out of the west like a bluebird?"

" 'Tis a winged foot that goes to meet a
friend," said the prince. "I left Rome far
behind you and I go to Jerusalem."

"We took you for a bandit."

"And I am only a king," said Antipater,
proudly. "I am summoned to take the
crown of my father."

"And is he dead?"

"Nay, but ill and weary of his burden."

Appius removed his helmet as he made
answer:

"The gods give you health, honor, and
wisdom, O king! Will you ride with us?"

"Already the gods give me honor," said
the prince, bowing politely as the troop
made way for him. "I doubt not they will
add health and wisdom. But there is a
blessing I put above either."

They started slowly, Antipater riding between Arria and her brother in advance of the troop.

"And shall we ask the gods to grant it?" said Arria.

"Yes, for it is your favor, sweet girl. I adore you, and shall have no other queen."

"I cannot give you my heart," said she, frankly. "It is impossible—I cannot bear to speak of it."

"And you would not share my power and glory with me?" said Antipater, turning, with a look of surprise.

Appius answered:

"Once before I have told you, my worthy prince, that whom the emperor chooses she will wed."

"Think not of that—I shall make terms with him," said Antipater. "She shall never wed a weak-hearted tribune."

"You speak lightly of my friend," said Appius. "I like it not, good sire."

"Son of Herod," said Arria, drawing

rein, " we cannot longer enjoy your company."

Appius halted the troop.

For a little Antipater was dumb with astonishment. He drew aside, and when he spoke his voice trembled with ire, it was near bursting into fury.

"Sweet girl," said he, caressing the neck of his horse, "not even the power of Rome shall forbid me to love you, and I swear, by the god of my fathers, no man shall live between us!" He turned quickly, and a fierce look came into his eyes and he added, in a hoarse half-whisper, "You shall be my wife, sister of Appius."

The young Roman wheeled his horse between them. Antipater backed away, threatening with his lance. He shouted to his trumpeter, his troop being hard by, and quickly a call sounded. Then spur went to flank, and the followers of the Jew passed in a quick rush and went thundering off, Antipater at the head of their column. He rode to Athens in ill humor

and was at Piræus three hours in advance
of Arria and Appius. The sun had set
and the sea lay calm in a purple dusk.
He went aboard his trireme at once and
called his pilot to him.

"Go find the vessel waiting here for one
Appius of Rome," he commanded.

"It is she that lies near us," said the
other.

"And you know her pilot?"

"Ay, 'tis Tepas the Idumæan. He knows
the broad sea as one may know his own
vineyard."

"Bring him to me."

When Tepas came, Antipater took him
aside and spread before him a chart of
the vast, purple sea which beat upon the
shores of Hellas. He put his finger on a
little spot some leagues from the coast of
Africa.

"Know you the Isle of Doom?" said he.

"Ay, 'tis a lonely heap of rocks."

"A roost of sea-birds," said the prince of
Judea. "Know you who am I?"

"You are the son of Herod."

"And I go to be king of the Jews."

Antipater took from a bag many pieces of gold and heaped them on the chart above the Isle of Doom.

"Would you earn this money, and much more?" he whispered.

"If you will but show me how," said Tepas, the fire of greed now burning in his heart.

"Sail close to the Isle of Doom. There your trireme shall be leaking and you shall desert her and seek refuge on the isle and wait for me. You shall have ample store of provisions, and this treasure, and when I come you shall have, also, three talents more and a home in Jerusalem, and my favor as long as you live."

"But how long must I wait?"

"Not beyond the ides of January, good man."

"Then I agree," said Tepas.

So was it with an evil man those days. If he were armed with power he halted not

198

between his plan and his purpose. There were, indeed, few things so valued as to be above price.

But the cunning of the tempter was to lead his prey into further depths of infamy. The prince took the hand of the sailor and whispered to him:

"If you would be a friend to me, then my enemies should be your enemies." He paused a moment, looking into the eyes of the pilot and tenderly patting his shoulder. It was like the guile of the black leopard. Presently he continued:

"Now this young Roman is my enemy. If by any chance he, Appius, should die before I come, you shall have six instead of three talents. He is fond of wine, and for such the sea has many perils. Do you understand me?"

"I do," said Tepas, nodding his approval, and then that heap of gold, lying on the chart, was delivered to him, and without more delay he went to his own vessel. Antipater sat in silence, thinking for a mo-

ment, his chin upon his breast. Soon the
thought of his enemies and their doom
brightened his eyes and lifted the corners
of his mouth a little and set his lips quivering. He leaned forward upon a table,
softly, as if in fear that some eye would
observe him. One might have heard then
that menacing, Herodian rumble in his
throat. He seemed to caress the table with
his hands.

"Dear Appius! Good Vergilius!" he muttered, seizing a piece of vellum and crushing it in his hand. "Soon my power shall
close upon you. And Arria, my pretty
maiden, you shall repair my heart with
kisses."

A pet kitten leaped upon the table. It
seemed to startle him, and he struck it dead
with his hand.

Then he sprang up suddenly and looked
about, a feline stealth upon him, and ran
with catlike paces to the deck.

"Get to work, you sea-rats!" he roared.
"Every man to his place. If we are not

gone to sea before the moon is up, some of you will be gone to Hades."

In half a moment slaves were up in the rigging and rushing across the deck and tumbling into the galley.

And that night Antipater pushed his prow into the deep sea.

Meanwhile Arria and Appius, fearing the power of this new king of Judea, and thinking also of the peril of Vergilius, travelled slowly, considering what they should do. Appius feared either to go or to return, but Arria was of better courage.

"I must go to him," said she. "You know not this love in me, dear brother. I would give up my life to be with him. If he is dead I shall never see the seven hills again. I shall go—" she paused, covering her eyes a moment.

"Where?"

"To the city of God," she whispered.

"May all the gods protect us," said her brother.

And the day after Antipater had set sail, they, too, with Cyran, the slave-girl, were moving southward in the great, middle sea.

GAIN the council of the covenant was in session. Herod, unknown to all, sat in the darkness of the council chamber. The intrigue of Salome and the treachery of Manius had led the Lion of Judea to his prey. Swords of fate were in the gloom that surrounded the traitors.

Now there had been, that night, a great discussion of the new king, and suddenly a man sitting by the side of Vergilius had risen. He began speaking in a strange voice, which had, however, some quality familiar to the young Roman. Shrill and

203

trembling with emotion, it thrilled many
with a feeling of religious awe.

"The time is upon us," said he, "when
the judges of the council have come to the
end of their deliberations. It is for me,
therefore, to reveal it to you in part. If
there be any here who give not full approval, let them freely express their
minds."

He did not explain that such were, then
and there, to be won by argument or put
out of the way by daggers.

"I speak of great things, but he that is
to follow me shall speak of greater. After
weighing all the promises of Holy Writ, and
enforcing their wisdom by the counsel of
other learned men," he continued, "your
judges declare the fulness of time."

The speaker paused. He heard a little
stir of bodies, a rustle of robes in the darkness.

The speaker went on:

"When Herod dies you shall see a rider
go swiftly through the streets bearing a red

banner and crying, 'The king is dead.'
Then shall the commander of the cohorts
go quickly and take possession of the royal
palace and await the new king."

Vergilius turned quickly in the direction
of the fateful voice. He had begun to suspect a plot. In a moment he saw to the
very depths of its cunning. Here was a
band of conspirators meeting in the darkness and speaking in disguised voices.
Probably no member had ever seen the
face of another, and the betrayal of a name
was, therefore, impossible. Vergilius, now
commander of the castle, heard with
consternation of his part in the pro-
gramme. By some movement of the speaker's body an end of his girdle was flung
against the hand of Vergilius. Imme-
diately the young Roman laid hold of the
silken cord. Tracing it stealthily, to make
sure of its owner, he drew his dagger and
cut the girdle in twain, hiding an end of it
in his bosom.

"The new king is in Rome," the speaker

added. "Presently you shall hear the voice of his herald, whose face I know not, but of whose fidelity and wisdom I have long been sure. He will give you further revelation of our purposes."

It was cunningly said, for the speaker knew that such a promise would delay the vengeance of Herod.

A little silence followed the ceasing of "the shrill voice." Vergilius could hear its owner moving away in the darkness. Fearful possibilities had begun to suggest themselves to the new convert. Now had he the flinty heart and the cunning mind of his fathers. The darkness had begun to smother and sicken him.

"Hear me now, good friends," said a low, calm, but unfamiliar voice, "and let my words enter your hearts and be there cherished in secret, for I shall tell you a name, and for its safe-keeping you shall answer to the Most High. Know you, then, that the new king is no other than the son of Herod and his name is Antipater—a man of great valor, learned in all wisdom and all mystery, who loves the people of God. His heart has suffered, feeling the wrongs of Israel. He has the voice of wrath, the hand of power, and the claim of a just and natural inheritor. I have his word that we who are bound in this council of the covenant shall share in the glory of his reign."

Vergilius, hot with anger, rose to his feet.

"Good sirs," said he, in a piping voice very unlike his own, "let us not approve without full understanding. There may be some here who in their zeal have been deceived. Let us be fair, and warn them that all who approve this plan are traitors. I came here to study the mysteries of the one God, and I am learning the mysteries of an evil plot. 'Tis a great surprise to me. I like it not, and shall have no part in it. I know not your names or your faces, but I know your plan is murder, and if the one God favor it, I can no longer honor Him."

He paused, but there came no answer. Again he heard a rustle of garments in the dark chamber, and, also, a stealthy and suggestive grating of steel upon scabbard. He perceived now the imminence of his peril. He could hear no sound in the darkness.

He stepped quickly aside, hearing not the feet which followed, nor feeling him who clung to the skirt of his toga. He stood silent, with dagger drawn. As he felt about him, he touched a pair of great, trembling hands. He stood motionless, expecting every breath to feel a point plunging into his flesh. Suddenly some one blew a sharp whistle close beside him. Then, for a little, it seemed as if the doors were being rent by thunderbolts. Crowding forms and cries of terror filled the darkness. The young Vergilius kept his place after the first outbreak. Men, rushing past him, had torn the toga from his back. The hands which had clung upon him now held his wrist with a grip immovable. Doors

fell and lights were flashing in. He saw
now, on every side, a gleam of helmet and
cuirass. Men, retreating from the lights,
huddled in a dark corner. Some began to
weep and cry to God. The scene was awful with swiftness and terror. The crowding group moved like caving sand. It
sank suddenly, every man going to his
knees. Quick as the serpent, a line of soldiers flung itself around them. Vergilius,
with the man who clung to him, stood
apart near the middle of the chamber.

Suddenly he heard an impatient, wrathful shout close beside him: "Lights here,
ye laggards!"

Vergilius jumped as if he had felt the
prick of steel. He turned, looking at the
man who held his arm. A squad with
torches came swiftly, forming about them.
The powerful hands let go; a cloak and
hood fell upon the floor.

"The king!" said Vergilius, bowing low.

"And you," said Herod, breathing heavily and leaning on the shoulder of the

young man, "you are the only friend of the king. To save you from the fate of those dogs yonder, I would not let you go."

This unloved and terrible man, still leaning upon the shoulder of Vergilius, wept feebly. It seemed as if the infirmity of old age had fallen suddenly upon him. He muttered, in a weak and piping tone, of his great life weariness. Then he seemed to hear those low cries of terror from beyond the line of guards. He lifted his head, listening. He turned quickly, crouching low, and seemed to threaten the soldiers near him with his hand. They stepped aside fearfully. Then was he, indeed, the old lion of Judea, ready to spring upon his prey.

"Stand them here before me," he growled, fiercely.

The conspirators were drawn up in line. Torches were held before their faces. Vergilius looked with pity at the terrified throng. There were Lugar and two merchants he knew, and that chamberlain of

Herod's palace who had taken him before
the king. There was also a famous young
Roman athlete, whom Vergilius had first
seen and admired at the circus in Rome,
and who had lately been a member of
the castle guard. But none wore the
girdle which Vergilius had cut in twain.

The king stood before them, raging like
a man possessed of demons. Fate, which
had whispered through lips of beauty in
the palace at Cæsarea, now thundered in
the voice of power.

"Serpents, murderers, children of the
devil!" he roared. "Soon shall your souls
wander in hell and your bodies rot in the
valley of Hinnom. Take them to the torture, and make it slow for such as give us no
further knowledge. Away with them! Let
their food be fear and their drink be the
sweat of agony and their end be death at
the games of Cæsar!"

The will of that graceful and voluptuous
maiden had been well if only partially
expressed.

A guard of soldiers led the unfortunate men away.

Herod, now weak and trembling, took the arm of Vergilius.

"To my palace!" said he, and they made their way to his litter.

"It will do no good to put them to torture," said Vergilius. "You have heard all. They have met in darkness and the leaders have disguised their voices. No member could be sure of the identity of any save himself. Only two or three, perhaps, could have betrayed other members of the order."

"Fool! were they not sure of Vergilius, the commander of the cohorts?" said Herod.

"But the plot is uncovered, and now, great sir, I implore you, try the remedy of Cæsar."

Herod ceased muttering and turned with a look of inquiry.

"Forgive them," Vergilius added.

The king answered with curses. Then from his chamber, where they had now ar-

rived, he drove all save the young Roman.
"Long ago I discovered evidence of the
treachery of the prince," said he. "To Antipater—foul son of Doris—I despatched
this letter."

He spread a sheet of vellum before Vergilius, bidding him read. It was the copy
of a letter addressed to his "dutiful and affectionate son Antipater." It recited that,
whereas he (Herod) was now become ill and
weary under his many cares, and needed
the companionship of them he loved, Antipater should ask, in the name of his
father, for a goodly escort of cavalry and
proceed at once to Jerusalem, there, shortly,
to receive his inheritance.

"Foul son of Doris!" the king growled,
hoarsely, as the young Roman turned.
Then his voice broke into a shrill, piping
laugh. "Ha, ha! He is coming—even now
he is coming to take the crown of his loving
father!"

Then he leaned forward with a savage
leer, as if he saw the object of his wrath.

His lips were parted, his mouth open, his breath came hissing from his throat.

"Foul son of Doris!" he repeated, beating the floor with his feet. "Your lies have drowned me in the blood of those I love. Swamp plant! creeping asp! Soon shall I put my foot upon you!"

Turning to Vergilius, he continued, presently:

"Be ready, my tribune, to go down to the sea with a cohort. There meet him, as he comes, and let him fall quickly from his height of greatness, and chain him, hand and foot, and bring him hence. You may go now."

Vergilius bowed and left the home of Herod. As he went away he fell to thinking of that girdle's end in his bosom. Although it was past the middle hour of night, he hastened to the palace of Manius. The assessor, distraught and pale, started as he met him, and Vergilius saw at once that an end of the other's girdle had been cut away. The young tribune drew that piece of braided silk from under his tunic.

"It is yours?" said he, tossing it to Manius.

"I—I had not observed," said the other, nervously. "It is part of the girdle I wear in deference to the people among whom I live. How came you by it?"

"Fox! Your cunning will not save you. Tell me first how you escaped the peril into which you had drawn me."

"I do not understand you."

"But I understand you," said Vergilius, with anger. "There are but two places in the world for you. One is beyond the boundaries of Rome, the other is the valley of Hinnom." Having said which, he turned, quickly, and left the assessor's palace.

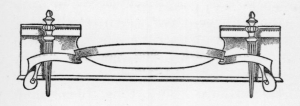

ARRIA and her brother were far from the shores of Hellas and near the Isle of Doom. Tepas knew that a few leagues more would bring him in sight of the familiar cliffs. Brother and sister were reclining on the deck of their trireme. The tenth day of their journey was near its end. The sun had sunk through misty depths of purple, and now seemed to melt and pour a flood of fire upon the waters.

"I am weary," said the girl, looking thoughtfully at the calm sea.

"Of me?" said her brother.

"Nay, but of that groaning of the rowers. It tells me of aching arms in the galley. I cannot sleep at night, hearing it."

Appius laughed with amusement. "Little fool!" said he. "The slaves of Tepas are all Jews."

"But they are men," said the beautiful girl; "and do you not understand, dear brother? I love a man."

"Love!" exclaimed Appius, with contempt. "'Tis only as the longing of the bird for its mate."

"Nay, I would give all for him I love."

"Not all," said he, with a look of surprise.

"Yes, all—even you, and my mother, and my home, and my country, and my life—I am sick with longing. And when I think of him I cannot bear to see men suffer."

"You are gone mad," said Appius, "and I pray the gods to bring you back. It may be the fair Vergilius forgets you."

She turned, quickly, and her voice trembled as she whispered: "Nay, he also has

the great love in him. He could not forget."

Cyran, the pretty slave-girl, came soon
with their evening repast. Arria bade her
sit beside them.

"Tell us, dear Cyran," said the Roman
beauty—"tell us a tale of old Judea."

"Beloved mistress," said Cyran, kneeling
by the side of Arria and kissing the border
of her robe, "listen; I will tell you of the
coming of the great love. Long ago there
was a maiden of Galilee so beautiful that
many came far to see her. Now, it so
befell, there came a certain priest, young
and fair to look upon, who did love her
and seek her hand in marriage. And
she loved him, even as you love, but
would not wed him. O my good mistress!
She knew that a mighty king was coming, and she was held of a great hope
that God would choose her for the blessed
mother. And, still loving the priest, she
kept herself pure in thought and deed.
Every day they saw each other, but stayed

apart, and their love grew holier the more it was put down. And oh, it was a wonder! for it filled their hearts with kindness and sent their feet upon errands of mercy. And many years passed, and one day they sat together.

"'My beloved, you are grown old and feeble, and so am I,' said she. 'We have pitied every child of sorrow but ourselves.' And they rose and put their arms about each other and went into the dark valley of death, heart to heart, that very day, and were seen no more of men. And they in the hills of Galilee, where the lovers dwelt, made much account of them, for while she had not borne the great king, still was she long remembered as the blessed mother of holy love. Now, maidens, with youth and love and beauty strong upon them, gave all for the great hope. And wonderful stories went abroad, and women were more sacred in the eyes of men, seeing that one of them, indeed, must be mother of the very Son of God."

The slave-girl covered her face and her body shook with emotion.

"Cyran, why are you crying?" said Arria.

"Because," Cyran replied, her voice trembling—"because I can never be the blessed mother."

"Tell me," said Arria, "have you never felt the great love?"

Cyran rose and looked down at her mistress.

"I have felt the pain of it," said she, sadly. "And my heart—Oh, it is like the house of mourning where Sorrow has hushed the Children of Joy. But the sweet pain of love is dear to me."

"Tell me of it."

"Good mistress, I cannot tell you."

"Why, dear Cyran?"

"Because—" the slave-girl hesitated; then timidly and with trembling lips she whispered, "because, dear mistress, I—I love you." She seemed to bend beneath her burden and knelt beside her mistress and wept.

220

"Go—please go," said Appius, turning to Cyran. "You irritate me, and I cannot understand you."

But Arria divined the secret of the poor slave-girl, and pitied her.

Cyran rose and left them.

"The great love may come to you, and then you shall understand," said Arria to Appius.

"The great madness!" her brother exclaimed. "I like not these Jewish cattle. The gods forgive me that we have fallen among them. With a Jew for a pilot we should make a landing in Hades."

Something in his manner alarmed the girl.

"What mean you?" she inquired.

"I will tell you to - morrow," said her brother. "'Tis time you went to your couch and I to mine. Have no fear."

Now, the young Roman had begun to suspect the pilot of some evil plan. After the girl had left him he sat drinking wine for hours. Soon he was in a merry way, singing songs and jesting with all who passed him. Long after the dark had come, when Tepas only remained upon deck, Appius reeled up and down, singing, with a flask in his hand. The moon had risen. Eastward her light lay like hammered silver on the ripples.

Appius neared the tall, rugged form of Tepas. Against the illumined waters he could see the long, bent nose, the great beard, the shaggy brows, the large, hairy head of his pilot. Tepas, who ruled his men with scourge and pilum, had made himself feared of all save the young Roman noble. Appius halted, looking scornfully at the Jew. Then he shouted:

"A knave, upon my honor! 'Tis better to be drunk, for then one has hope of recovery. You long-haired dog! Here is something would make you bay the moon. Drink and howl. You weary me with silence."

Tepas, familiar with the contempt of Romans, took the flask, and, pouring into

his cup, drank of the rich wine. Then
Appius held the flask above his head, and
with a word of scorn flung it into the sea.
He started to cross the deck and fell heavily.
Now, after striving, as it seemed, to regain
his feet, he lay awhile muttering and helpless and soon began to snore. The deck
was deserted by all save him and the pilot.
Tepas looked down at the young Roman.
Already, far off in the moonlight, he had
seen cliffs and knew they were on the Isle of
Doom. He must be about his business.
He went to where Appius lay and bent
over him. The pilot drew his dagger; the
youth rolled drowsily and his hands were
now upon the feet of Tepas. The latter
leaned to strike. A sound startled him.
It was a footfall close behind. The Jew
rose, turning to listen. Suddenly his feet
went from under him and he fell headlong; quickly two seamen leaped upon
him, seizing his head and hands. One
disarmed him, the other covered his
mouth. Appius clung upon the feet of

the Jew. A Roman slave had taken the wheel.

"Shall we bind him?" said one of the seamen.

"No," said Appius, breathing heavily as the pilot tried to shake him off. "Give the dog a chance. Yonder is an island. We shall soon be near it, and by swimming he may save his life."

"The gold is upon him," said a seaman; "I can feel it under his tunic."

"But we shall not rob him," was the answer of Appius.

"It is heavy. It will be like a stone to sink him."

"However, we shall not rob him," the young Roman repeated.

Now, when they were come as near the isle as they dare bring their ship, Appius gave a command. They lifted the body of that cursing wretch. Back and forth they swung it as one counted. Then over it went with reaching hands and fell upon the moonlit plane of water. They could see him rise and turn towards the isle, swimming. Weighted by his burden, he swam not twice his length before the sea closed above him.

"I thought he had struck you with his dagger," said one of the seamen.

"It would have done no harm," Appius replied. "I have a corselet under my tunic. Is the ship still leaking?"

"A little, good sire. We found a wedge in the planks. He would have driven it through, no doubt, if all had gone well with him. I know not why, unless he meant to beach her under the cliffs yonder."

The young Roman stood silent for a little time. Presently his thought came in a whisper to his lips: "And hold my sister until Antipater should come."

He called the seamen to his side.

"I, who am a friend of the great father of Rome," said he, "shall see you well rewarded. The little I gave you is not enough. Without your help and warning worse luck than death might soon have come to us."

A light wind was now blowing, and the sails began to fill.

Suddenly all rushed forward, falling upon the deck. Their trireme had lost half her headway and was now crashing over rocks and trembling as her bow rose. She stopped, all her timbers groaning in the shock, and rolled sideways and lay with tilted deck above the water. Cries of alarm rose from her galley. Men fought their way up the ladders and scrambled like dripping rats to every place of vantage. After the shock, Appius had leaped to the upper rail, and, rushing forward to the door of Arria's deck-house, found her and the slave-girl within it, unharmed. The two were crying with fear, and he bade them dress quickly and await his orders. Then he took command. Soon a raft and small boats were ready alongside the wreck. Within half an hour Appius and the two maidens and part of the crew landed.

Before daylight all were safely carried to
the bare, lonely rocks, with a goodly store
of food and water.

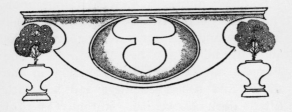

# Chapter

## 22

T was a clear morning and
the tenth day before the
kalends of January. Since
the ides, Vergilius had been
lying in camp with a co-
hort, near the port of Ascalon. Night and day on
the headland velites had been watching for
the trireme of Antipater. A little before
dawn their beacon - fires had flamed up.
Since daylight all had been watching the far-
come vessel of the son of Herod, and, as she
came near, they could see the pattern of
gold upon the royal vestments of Antipater.
Now, presently, he would set foot upon the
unhappy land of his inheritance. The co-

hort had formed in a long arc at the landing.
Before now, on his return, the king's horsemen had greeted him with cheers; to-day
he greeted them with curses. Vergilius,
hard by, faced the cohort, his back turned
to the new-comer. Antipater halted as he
came ashore, looking in surprise at the
tribune. He seized a lance, and, crouching
as he ran, with sly feet approached the
Roman officer. He was like the cat nearing
its prey. Vergilius, now seeming unmind-
ful of his pursuer, walked in the direction of the cohort. Swiftly, stealthily, the
prince came near, intending to plunge his
lance into the back of the young tribune.
Suddenly there rose an outcry among the
soldiers. Vergilius turned; the prince halted, breathing heavily, for he had run near
a hundred paces in the sea-sand. A roar of
rage burst from his lips.

"Dog!" he shouted. "Bid them cheer
me or I will run you through!" His lance
threatened.

"There shall be cheers in a moment, son

of Herod," said Vergilius, calmly and respectfully approaching him. Antipater, unaware of his peril, stood with lance at rest. With a hand quick as the paw of a leopard, Vergilius whirled it away and caught the wrist of the Jew and flung him down. While Antipater struggled in his great robe the tribune had disarmed him. Every man of the cohort was now cheering. Antipater rose in terrible wrath and flung off his robe of gold and purple.

"Put him in irons!" he shouted. "I, who shall soon be king of the Jews, command you!"

The cohort began to jeer at him; Vergilius commanded silence.

"You lapdog!" Antipater hissed, turning upon the Roman. "Am I met with treason?"

"You give yourself a poor compliment," said Vergilius. "Better call me a lion than a lapdog." He turned to an officer who stood near and added: "You will now obey the orders of the king."

230

Forthwith, Vergilius went aboard the new-come vessel and seized the goods of Antipater and put them on their way to the king. Meanwhile, the soldiers, many of whom had borne with the cruelty and insolence of their prisoner, were little inclined to mercy. He struggled, cursing, but they bore him down, binding him hand and knee to an open litter, so he stood, like a beast, upon all fours, for such, indeed, was the order of the king. Then they put on him the skin of a wild ass and carried him up and down, jeering as the long ears flapped. Vergilius, returning, removed the skin of the ass and loosed the fetters a little, and forbade the soldiers any further revenge.

"The skin of a leopard would become you better," said Vergilius to Antipater, as he unlashed the coat of shame.

The wrathful Jew, still cursing, tried to bite the friendly hand of his keeper. "My noble prince," said Vergilius, "you flatter me; I am not good to eat."

Those crowding near laughed loudly, but

Vergilius hushed them and signalled to the trumpeter. Then a call and a rush of horses into line. The litter was lifted quickly and lashed upon the backs of two chargers. In a little time the cohort was on its way to Jerusalem.

Arriving, it massed in front of the royal palace. Vergilius repaired to the king's chamber. The body of Herod was now become as an old house, its timbers sagging to their fall, its tenant trembling at dim windows while the storm beat upon it. Shame and sorrow and remorse were racking him down. King and kingdom were now swiftly changing.

"At last!" he piped, with quivering hands uplifted. "Slow - footed justice! come — come close to me."

Eagerly he grasped the hands of the young Roman and kissed them. Then he spoke with bitter irony, his words coming fast. "You met the great king?"

"Yes, good sire."

"You put him in chains and brought him hither?"

"And I commend him to your mercy."

"Ha, ha!" the king shrieked, caressing the hand of the Roman. Now his head rose, and for a little his old vigor and menacing voice returned to him. "He has run me through with the blade of remorse and put upon me the chains of infirmity," he complained, an ominous, croaking rattle in his throat. "To-day, to-day, my wrath shall descend upon him and my gratitude upon you! These forty years have I been seeking a man of honor. At last, at last, here is the greatest of men! I, Herod, surnamed the Great, king of Judea, conqueror of hosts, builder of cities, bare my head before you!"

He removed his jewelled crown; he drew off his purple tarboosh, and bowed before the young tribune. Tenderly Vergilius replaced them on the gray head.

"O king," said he, bowing low, "you do me great honor."

Herod closed his eyes and muttered feebly. Again remorse and age had flung their weight upon him. His hard face seemed to shrink and wither, and the young man thought as he looked upon it, "What a great, good thing is death!"

The king opened his eyes and piped, feebly: "Help me; help me to win the favor of my people! You shall be procurator, commander of the forces, counsellor of kings, priest of God."

The king waited, but Vergilius made no reply. Now, indeed, was he living in a great and memorable moment. He thought of the power offered him—power of doing and undoing, power of raising up and putting down, power over good and evil.

"Well," said Herod, impatiently, "what say you?"

"O king!" said Vergilius, "I had hoped soon to return to Rome and marry and live in the land of my fathers."

"Hear me, good youth," said Herod, sternly, seizing the hand of the young man. "There is a wise proverb in Judea. It is: 'Speak not much with a woman.' Had I

234

obeyed it, then had I saved my soul and
happiness. Women have been ever false
with me — an idle, whispering, and mis-
chievous crew! O youth, give not your
heart to them! For five years let Judea
be your bride. She woos you, son of Varro,
and she is fair. She asks for love and justice, and she will give you immortal fame."

The king fondly pressed the hand of the
Roman, who stood beside him, grave and
thoughtful. For the young man it was a
moment of almost overwhelming temptation. Love and ambition wrestled in his
soul. He stood silent.

"For only five years," the king pleaded.
"For five years give me your heart. Man!"
he shouted, impatiently, "will you not
answer?"

"I will consider," said Vergilius, calmly.

"Go!" said Herod, in a burst of ire.
Then, presently: "Now, now I will attend
to the son of Doris."

And Vergilius hastened away.

Within the hour, Antipater, son of Herod

the Great, was dragged to that strong chamber in a remote end of the vast home of Herod whence were to come cries for mercy by night such as he had often heard from his own victims.

## Chapter

### 23

OW in Vergilius and in many of that time the human heart had dropped its plummet into new depths of feeling, the human mind had made a reach for nobler principles. A greater love between men and women, spreading mysteriously, had been as the uplift of a mighty wave on the deep of the spirit. It had broadened the sympathy of man; it had extended his vision beyond selfish limits. Vergilius and Arria had crossed the boundary of barbaric evolution under the leadership of love. The young man was now in the borderland of

new attainment. He was full of the joy
and the wonder of discovery. He was like
a child—eager for understanding and impatient of delay. Now he thought with the
pagans and now with the Jews.

At his palace a letter had been waiting
for the tribune. It was from his friend
Appius. "My excellent and beloved Vergilius," it said, "I address you with a feeling
of deep concern for your safety. To-night
by tabellarius, my letter shall go down to
the sea on its way to Jerusalem. And now
to its subject. This morning I went to the
public games, and, returning, I was near my
palace when a messenger, bearing the command of Augustus, overtook and stopped
me. Quickly I made my way to The Laurels.
Our great imperator was in his chamber and
reading letters. He gave me a glance and
greeted me. I saw he wished me to come
near, and I stood close beside him. Then,
with that slow, gentle tone, he hurled his
lightning into me—you remember his way.
He told me, as he read, that you were mak-

238

ing rapid progress in Jerusalem; that you
had become a conspirator, a prophet, and
were likely soon to be an angel. And he
bade me go to you with his congratulations
that you have succeeded so long in keeping
your head upon your shoulders. Oh, deep
and cunning imperator! Said he: 'I cannot
tell you the name of my informant; and
really, my good son, why—why should I?'
There, spread before me on the table, so I
knew he wished me to see it, was a letter
which bore the signature of Manius and
gave information of a certain council. I
could not make out the name, but I was
able to recall how the great father had
said to me, once, that when a man secretly
puts blame upon another, the infamy he
charges shall be only half his own. Our
imperator is no fool, my friend. 'A ship
will be leaving the seventh day before the
ides,' said he. '*You* will not be able to make
it.' His meaning was clear. It could bear
my warning, if not me, and here it is. With
the gods' favor, soon, also, I shall be able

to say to you, here am I. To-morrow at dawn I leave for Jerusalem."

Beneath the signature these words were added: "As soon as possible I wish to know all and to speak my heart to you. The emperor has withdrawn his consent to your marriage with Arria. I shall explain everything but the purpose of the emperor, and who may understand him? If it be due to caprice or doubt or anger he will do you justice. But if a deeper motive is in his mind who knows what may happen?"

This letter kindled a fire in the heart of Vergilius. It burned fiercely, so that prudence and noble feeling were driven out. In spite of the warning of the young tribune, Manius had remained in Jerusalem. Vergilius had delayed action, dreading to bring the wrath of Rome upon one so young, so well born, so highly honored, and possibly so far misled. Therefore, he had held his peace and waited patiently for more knowledge. Now the evil heart of the assessor was laid bare, his infamy proven. Vergilius reread the letter with flashing eyes. Then he summoned his lecticarii and set out for the palace of the plotter. Manius approached him, a kindly greeting on his lips.

"Liar!" Vergilius interrupted, his hand upon his sword. "Speak no word of kindness to me!"

"What mean you, son of Varro?" the other demanded.

"That, with me, you have not even the right of an enemy. You are a deadly serpent, born to creep and hide. Shame upon you — murderer! If there be many like you, what—God tell me!—what shall be the fate of Rome?"

Vergilius stepped away, and, lifting his hands, gave the other a look of unspeakable scorn. Manius made no reply, but stood as still and white as marble, with sword in hand.

"It was I who sat beside you that night," said the other, his voice aglow with feeling.

"When I heard you speak treason I cut off the end of your girdle. But you left by some unguarded way and escaped the fate of your fellows. You have not seen them since, and shall not. When you see them die in the arena think what you escaped, although deserving it more than they. Vile serpent! you brought the king, and hoped to send me also to Hades. You are a traitor, and that I know. Traitor to friend and country! Dare to provoke me further and I shall slay you!"

"What would you, son of Varro?" said the other, sullenly.

"Wretch! If you would save your life, hide as becomes the asp. Creep away from them who would put their feet upon you. Go live and die with the wild men of the far deserts."

"Traitor to the gods!" said Manius, threatening with his sword. "Roman Jew! I am of noble birth, and claim the right of combat."

"I give it, though you have no better

242

right than dogs. Well, it would please my
hand to slay you. I know the name and
father you have dishonored, and you are
grandnephew of the good Lady Claudia—
noble mother of Publius. For their sake I
give you the right of combat. By the way-
side near Bethlehem are lonely hills. There,
the seventh day before the kalends, in the
middle hour of the night, you shall see a
beacon-fire and near it my colors. Three
friends may go with each, and you and I
will draw swords in the fire-light.''

"I shall meet you there," said Manius.

Vergilius, putting away his weapon,
turned quickly, and, without speaking, left
the traitor's palace with firm faith in the
one God—that he was ever on the side of
the just who humbly sought his favor.

# Chapter

## 24

HE festival of games, in honor of Augustus, were about to begin at Cæsarea. Lately the highway from north to south, which passed the gates of Jerusalem, had been as a fair of the nations. A host had journeyed far to amuse the great king or to enjoy his holiday. Gayer and more given to proud speech than they who came to the festivals of the Temple, beneath the skullbone there was yet a more remarkable unlikeness.

These were mostly the children of Hatred, each heart a lair of wild passions, each brain

teeming with catlike gods. Here were
they to be lifted up by the power of love—
the heathen, the debased. What a gathering of the enemies of God and man! Crowding at the gates were gladiators from
Greece and Rome; Arab chiefs upon camels,
with horses trained for the race; troops of
rich men with armed retainers; hunters
bringing wild beasts in cages lashed upon
heavy carts; squads of Roman cavalry;
gamblers, peddlers, thieves, bandits, musi-
cians, dancers, and singers, some walking,
some riding horse or camel. Many had
travelled far for one purpose—to behold the
great king. Now solemn whispers of gossip
had gone to every side of the city. Herod
was ill, so said they, and had not long to
live. That morning of the day before the
games the old king had summoned Vergilius.

"I will not be cheated by God or man,"
said he, fiercely. "Tell the master of the
games that I will have him entertain me
here to-day, after the middle hour, in my

palace court. Bid him bring beast and gladiator and the strong men of the prisons. Let him not forget the traitors. I would have, also, a thousand maids to sing and dance for me."

The king looked down, impatiently, at his trembling hands. He flung a wrathful gesture, and again that bestial voice: "Go, bid him bring them!"

So at the middle hour a wonderful scene was beginning in the great court of Herod's palace. The king sat on a balcony with Salome, Elpis, Roxana, Phædra, and others of his kindred. On the circular terraces of a great fountain below and in front of them were rows of naked maidens. Circle after circle of this living statuary towered, with diminishing radii, above the court level, to an apex, where a stream of cool, perfumed water, broken to misty spray, rose aloft, scattering in the sunlight. So cunningly had they contrived to enhance the charm of the spectacle, those many graceful shapes were under a fine, transparent veil of water-drops lighted by rainbow gleams and sweet with musky odor. Circles were closely massed around the base of the fountain. They stood in silence, all looking down. The old king surveyed them. Within the palace a hundred harpers smote their strings, flooding the scene with music. Slowly each circumference began to move. Step and measure increased their speed. The circles were now revolving, one around another, with swift and bewildering motion. At a signal the silent figures broke into song. They sang of the glories of Jerusalem and the great king. Herod's hand was up — he would have no more of it. The song ceased, the circles, one by one, rolled into helices which, unbending into slender lines, vanished quickly beneath a great arch. Then a trumpet peal and a rattle of iron wheels. Brawny arms were pushing a movable arena. Swiftly it came into that ample space between the king and the great fountain. Behind its iron bars a large lion

paced up and down. Two hundred mounted men of the cohort stood in triple rank
some fifty paces from the scene. Vergilius,
on a white charger, was in front of the
column.

While Arab slaves pushed the arena into
place, David came and touched the arm of
the young tribune. He whispered, eagerly:
"My sister, Cyran the Beloved, is here.
She is waiting at the castle."

"Whence came she?" said the tribune,
with astonishment.

"From the port of Ascalon, where she
arrived by trireme with Appius. They
were wrecked, finding shore in a far country.
There the friend of Cæsar, Probus Sulpicius
Quirinus, discovered them on his way from
Carthage, and brought them hither."

Appius, fearing Antipater, had waited by
the sea while Cyran came to find her
brother and Vergilius. The prince's threat
and the words of Cæsar had checked his
feet with caution. He forbade Cyran to
tell any one of the presence of Arria.

"And where is my friend?" Vergilius demanded.

"He waits on the ship to hear from you —whether it be safe to come. It seems Antipater has threatened him."

"Tell Cyran I would have her come to me. Then find my orderly and bid him bring Appius hither by the way of Bethlehem. If he arrives there before the end of the third watch he will see my fire-light on the hill."

David left the scene as a powerful Thracian, standing by the arena's gate, saluted the king. Entering, the gladiator engaged the lion with his lance. Incautiously he pressed his weapon too far, drawing blood. Before he could set his lance the wild foe was upon him. A leap into the air, a double stroke of the right fore-paw, and down fell the beast, while the man reeled, with rent tunic, and caught the side of the arena. In a twinkling, as he clung feebly, he reddened from head to toe. Three bestiarii had thrust in their lances and held the lion back; others opened a gate and removed the dying gladiator. Herod, leaning over, beckoned to the master of the games.

"A noble lion!" said he, his voice trembling. "Save him for the battle of the pit."

Now, in pursuance of the order of the king, a pit had been dug and walled with timber near that place where the fighter had met his death. A score of slaves forthwith lowered the arena into the pit with ropes. Herod and all who sat with him could see the open top of the barred space, but the beast was beyond their vision.

Another trumpet-call. A band of prisoners have entered the court. Antipater, tall and erect in exomis of plain gray, right arm and shoulder bare, walked in the centre of the front rank. Traitors of the betrayed council were there beside him. Slowly they about to die came forth and stood in even rank and bowed low before the king. Herod beat his palms upon the

golden rail before him and muttered hoarsely. Then with raised finger and leering
face he taunted them.

"Outlaws!" he croaked. "I doubt not ye
be also cowards."

All drew back save Antipater and a huge
Scythian bandit. They drew broadswords
and rushed together, fighting with terrific
energy. The Scythian fell in a moment.
One after another four conspirators came
to battle with their chief, but each went
down before his terrible attack. Some
asked for mercy as they fell, but all perished
by the hand of him they had sought to
serve. Held for the battle of the pit, the
young Roman whom Vergilius had rec-
ognized in the council chamber advanced
to meet Herod's son. He had won his
freedom in the arena and lost it in the
conspiracy of the prince. He was a tall,
lithe, splendid figure of a man. The heart
of the young commander was touched with
pity as he beheld the comely youth. This
game, invented by Antipater himself, was

251

a test of strength and quickness. Nets
were the only weapons, strong sinews and a
quick hand the main reliance of either.
Each tried to entangle the other in his net
and secure a hold. Then he sought to rush
or drag his adversary to the edge of the pit
and force him down. Weapons lay on
every side of the arena below. The unfortunate had, therefore, a chance to defend
himself against the lion.

On the signal to begin, Jew and Roman
wrestled fiercely, their weapons on their
arms, but neither fell. Suddenly Antipater
broke away and flung his net. Nimbly the
other dodged. Down came the net, grazing
his head. Swiftly he sprang upon the Jew,
striving to entangle him. Antipater pulled
away. Again the Roman was upon his
enemy and the two struggled to the very
noses of the cohort. Hard by the centre
of the column, where sat Vergilius on his
charger, the powerful prince threw his adversary, and, choking him down, secured
the net over his head. Swiftly he began

to drag the fallen youth. Vergilius, angered by the prince's cruelty, could no longer hold his peace.

"'Tis unfair," said he, pointing at Antipater. "In the name of the fatherly Augustus, I protest."

The prince, still dragging his foe, answered with insulting threats. The young commander leaped from his horse and ran to the side of Antipater. The latter released his captive and drew sword. Swiftly Vergilius approached him and the two met with a clash of steel.

Now the first battle in that war of the spirit, which was to shake the world with fury had begun.

Back and forth across the court of Herod they fought their way—the son of light and the son of darkness. Sparks of fire flew from their weapons while a murmur in the cohort grew to a loud roar and the old king and his women stood with hands uplifted shrieking like fiends of hell. Hand and foot grew weary; their speed slackened. Slowly, now, they moved in front of the cohort and back to the middle space. They were evenly matched; both began to reel and labor heavily, their strength failing in like degree. The end was at hand. Now the angel of death hovered near, about to choose between them. Suddenly Antipater, pressing upon his man, fell forward. At the very moment Vergilius, who had been giving quarter, reeled a few paces and was down upon his back. Prince and tribune lay apart some twenty cubits. Both tried to rise and fell exhausted. Half a moment passed. Antipater had risen to his elbow. Slowly he gained a knee, while the other lay as one dead. He rested, staring with vengeful eyes at his enemy. Stealthily he felt for his weapon. The right hand of Vergilius began to move. A hush fell upon the scene. Swiftly, from beside the cohort a fair daughter of Judea, in a white robe, ran across the field of battle. She knelt beside Vergilius and touched his pale face with her hands. * Then she called to him: "Rise,

O my beloved! Rise quickly! He will slay you!"

"Cyran!" he whispered.

Antipater had gained his feet and now ran to glut his anger. Cyran rose upon her knees and put her beautiful body between the steel and him she loved. The sword seemed to spring at her bosom. She seized it, clinging as if it were a thing she prized. Vergilius had risen. Swiftly sword smote upon sword. The young Roman pressed his enemy, forcing him backward. From dying lips he heard again the old chant of faith:

"Let me not be ashamed—I trust in Thee, God
   of my fathers;
Send, quickly send the new king" . . .

The words seemed to strengthen his arm. He fought as one having power above that of men. On and on he forced his foe with increasing energy. He gave him no chance to stop or turn aside. Yells of fury drowned the clash of steel. The tumult

grew. The son of Herod was near the pit.
He seemed to tempt the Roman to press
him. Suddenly he leaped backward to the
very edge. The Roman rushed upon him.
Before their swords met, Antipater sprang
aside with the quickness of a leopard. In
cunning he had outdone his foe. Unable
to check his onrush, Vergilius leaped forward and fell out of sight. A booming
roar from the startled lion rose out of the
pit and hushed the tumult of the people.
Herod, pointing at his son, shrieked with
rage as he bade the soldiers of the cohort to
seize and put him in irons.

A score of slaves hastened to the mouth
of the pit. They caught the ropes and
quickly lifted the arena. As it came into
view the tumult broke out afresh. There,
far spent, resting on his bloody weapon,
near the middle of the arena stood Vergilius,
and the lion lay dead before him.

Slaves opened the iron gate. Vergilius
ran to the still form of the slave-girl. He
knelt beside her and kissed her lifeless hand.

"Poor child of God!" he whispered. "If indeed you loved me, I have no wonder that you knelt here to die."

The master brought a wreath of laurel to the young tribune, saying: "'Tis from the king." Vergilius seemed not to hear. Tenderly he raised the lifeless body of Cyran in his arms. The spectators were cheering. "Hail, victor!" they shouted.

"Hail, victor!" he whispered, looking into the dead face. "Blessed be they who conquer death."

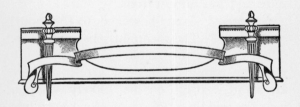

HE day was near its end. Soldiers of the cohort, bearers of the dead, harpers and singers filed through the gate of Herod's palace. Hard by, in Temple Street, were many people. An old man stood among them, his white beard falling low upon a purple robe, his face turned to the sky. He sang as if unconscious of all around him. Often he raised his hand, which trembled like a leaf in the wind. Horses, maidens, and men halted to hear the words:

"Now is the day foretold of them who dwell in the dust of the vineyard.

258

# Vergilius

Bow and be silent, ye children of God and ye of
    far countries.
Consider how many lie low in the old, imme-
    morial vineyard.
Deep—fathom deep—is the dust of the dead
    'neath the feet of the living.

"Gone are they and the work of their hands—
    all save their hope and desire have per-
    ished.
Only the flowers of the heart have endured—
    only they in the waste of the ages.
Ay—they have grown, but the hewn rock has
    crumbled away and the temples have fallen.
Bow, haughty people; ye live in the day of
    fulfilment—the day everlasting.
Soon the plough of oppression shall cease and
    the ox shall abandon the furrow.
Ready the field, and I sing of the sower whose
    grain has been gathered in heaven.

"Now is he come, with my voice and my soul I
    declare him.
Wonderful Counsellor, Mighty God, the Ever-
    lasting Father, the Prince of Peace."

The flood of inspiration had passed. The
singer turned away. "It is Simeon," said
a voice in the crowd. "He shall not die

until his eyes have beheld the king of promise."

Those departing from the games of Herod resumed their march. At the gate of the castle of Antonia, Vergilius, with David and two armed equites, one bearing colors, left the squadron. They rode slowly towards the setting sun. Now there was not in all the world a city so wonderful as Jerusalem. Golden dome and tower were gleaming above white walls on the turquoise blue of the heavens.

"Good friend, I grieve for her who is dead," said Vergilius to David.

"She died for love," the other answered as one who would have done the same.

Vergilius looked not to right nor left. His dark, quivering plume was an apt symbol of thought and passion beneath it. His blood was hot from the rush and wrath of battle, from hatred of them who had sought his life. He could hear the cry of Cyran: "Rise, rise, my beloved!" Again, he was like as he had been there on the field of battle. He could not rise above his longing for revenge. He hated the emperor whose cruel message had wrung his heart; he hated Manius, who had sought to destroy him; he despised the vile and stealthy son of Herod, who had plotted to rob him of love and life; he had begun to doubt the goodness of the great Lawgiver.

No sooner had he found an enemy than his God was become a god of vengeance. The council, the continued failure of his prayers, the cruelty of impending misfortune, the death of Cyran had weakened the faith of Vergilius. He had begun to founder in the deep mystery of the world. The voice of the old singer had not broken the spell of bitter passion. Vergilius trembled with haste to kill. He feared even that his anger would abate and leave him unavenged. There were memories which bade him to forgive, and of them was the gentle face of Arria, but he turned as one who would say "Begone!" He had not time even to consider what he should do to oppose the will of the emperor. As they rode on, his companion addressed the young commander.

"Saw you Manius in the balcony of Herod?"

"No."

"As I passed beneath it I saw him by the side of Salome, and I heard her say: 'Not until you slay him shall I be your wife.' I fear she means you ill, good friend."

"She-cat!" exclaimed Vergilius. "'Tis a yowling breed that haunts the house of Herod."

They came soon to where a throng was gathered thick, so for a little they saw not a way to pass. In the midst were three men sitting upon tall, white camels, their trappings rich with colored silk and shining metal.

"They speak to the people," said David. "It must be their words are as silver and gold."

"I doubt not they be story-tellers from the desert," said one behind.

The press parted; the camels had begun to move slowly. One of their riders hailed the young commander, saying, in a voice that rang like a trumpet:

"Where is he that is born king of the Jews?"

"I would I knew," was the answer of Vergilius.

"So shall ye soon," said the stranger. "We have seen his star in the east and have come to worship him."

The camels passed with long, stately strides. The horsemen resumed their journey.

"Strange!" thought Vergilius, turning his charger and looking back. "They be surely those who have travelled far."

The squad of cavalry, under plume and helmet, moved on, passing the Joppa gate and riding slowly down a long hill.

"See the glowing clouds yonder," said Vergilius, pointing westward.

"Ay, they be fair as the tents of Kedar," was the answer of David.

263

There is a great beauty in the sky and the blue hills," Vergilius remarked, thoughtfully.

"And you would kill, look not upon them—they are so fair."

"If I close my eyes, then, I do see a thing more fair."

"What?"

"The face of one I love. It is a love greater than all other things—fame or king or fatherland."

"Or revenge?" inquired David.

For a little Vergilius made no answer; but presently he said: "I am a Roman; who seeks my life shall lose his own."

They came upon a ewe lying in the roadway. She looked up with a mute appeal, but moved not. She seemed to reckon upon the kindness of them approaching. The squad parted, passing on either side. All drew rein, and one, dismounting, stood a moment looking down at her. Then laying hold of her fleece, he moved the ewe tenderly aside.

"A sign and a wonder!" said the Roman knight, as they continued their journey. "That old fighter has no hand for kindness."

"But mark this miracle of God," said the friend of Vergilius. "He softens the heart of those with young and makes gentle the hand that touches them. Ay, has he not softened the heart of the world? 'Tis like a mother whose time is near."

Soon a purple dusk had overflooded the hills and risen above the splendor of Jerusalem. The old capital was now like a dim, mysterious, golden isle in a vast, azure sea. Vergilius thought, as he went on, of those camel-riders. He seemed to hear in the lift and fall of hoofs, in the rattle of scabbards, that strange cry: "Where is he that is born king of the Jews?"

Darkness fell upon those riding in silence on the lonely road. Suddenly they drew rein, listening.

Said Vergilius, whispering: "I thought I heard voices."

"And I," said David, his words touched

with awe. " 'Twas like tens of thousands singing in some distant place."

Again they listened, but the song, if song it was, had ceased.

Then, boldly, as one who would put down his fear, the color-bearer spoke up: " 'Tis a band of shepherd folk on some far hill. Never saw I so dark a night. By the curtains of Solomon, I cannot see my horse!"

"There is no star in the sky," said another.

Then said the young commander, whist with awe: "Look yonder! A light on the hills! I saw it appear."

Amazement was in the tone of David: "Nay, 'tis a window of paradise! Or maybe that time is come when the three great stars should gather side by side. Do you not remember the talk of the astrologers?"

"I say 'tis a light on the hills." Vergilius now spoke in a husky, solemn whisper. "See, 'tis larger; and I would think it near the village of Bethlehem."

After a moment of silence he added, with a laugh: "Why stand we here and whisper, like a lot of women? Let us move on."

Again he seemed to hear peals of song in the sky and their rhythm in hoof and scabbard. It put him in mind of that strange, mysterious chant of the old singer.

Soon he drew rein, saying: "Halt and listen!" They stopped, conscious only of the great silence of the night. Vergilius felt for the arm of his friend.

"What think you?" said he, his voice full of wonder. "I doubt not the sound is in our fancy."

"See! The star! It grows!" said David, eagerly. " 'Tis like a mighty lantern hung in the dome of the sky."

Then said Vergilius, a pagan fancy filling his mind: "It may be God is walking upon the earth."

A moment they rode on, looking up at the heavens. Suddenly Vergilius bade them halt again, saying: "Hist! What is that cry?"

Now they could hear a faint halloo far behind them.

Then the bearer of the colors remarked: "It might be the squad of Manius."

"God curse him!" said Vergilius, quickly, his heart filling with passion dark as the night around. He heard no more the great song, but only the smite of steel in deadly combat. He seemed to see his enemy fall bleeding at his feet. "I will take what Herod offers," he thought. "I will make war on the cats and the serpents."

He had forgotten everything now save his bitterness.

"See! 'Tis gone!" said his friend, in a loud whisper. "The star is gone! I saw it disappear as if a cloud were suddenly come over it."

All drew rein, looking into the sky. Many stars were now uncovered in the vault above them.

" 'Twas a light on the hills," said Vergilius, with a vague fear in him. "Yon-

der I can see a smaller one.   'Tis a lantern.
Look!  It moves."

Suddenly they were startled by a mighty
voice that seemed to travel far into dark
and lonely caverns of the sky.  Like a
trumpet-call it resounded over the gloomy
hills—that cry of the camel-rider:

"Where is he that is born king of the
Jews?"

Vergilius whispered, his awe returning:
"They are coming—those men who rode
the camels."

Said David, his voice trembling: "They
are like many who have gone abroad with
that ancient hope in them."

The horsemen now stood, breathing low
as they listened.   Vergilius was full of wonder, thinking of the awe which had fallen
upon him and the others.   He tried to
throw it off.  "We waste time," said he,
starting his charger.  "Come, good men,
we have work to do."

Awhile they rode in silence, their eyes
on the light of the lantern.  Slowly they

came near, and soon saw its glow falling
upon rocks and moving shadows beneath it.

Then said David, turning to Vergilius:
"The battle — suppose it goes ill with
you?"

"Ill!" said the Roman, with rising ire.
"Then Jehovah is no better than Mars."

They could now see people standing in
the light of a lantern which hung above the
entrance of a cave.  Its opening was large
enough to admit a horse and rider.

"Soldiers of Cæsar!"—the whisper went
from mouth to mouth there in the light of
the lantern.

The horsemen halted.

"I shall soon be done with this traitor
to friend and king," thought the tribune,
dismounting and approaching the cave.

That group of people under the light, seeing symbols of Roman authority and hearing its familiar voice, fell aside with fear in
their faces.  A woman standing in the entrance of the cave addressed Vergilius, her
voice trembling with emotion.

270

"Good sir," said she, "if you mean harm
to those within I pray you go hence."

"I know not who is within," he answered,
as both he and David passed her. Fearing treachery, they drew their swords. Just
beyond the entrance of the cave both
halted. A man stood before them, his
face full of high authority, his hand
raised as if to command silence. He
was garbed like a toiler and somewhat
past middle age, his beard and eyebrows
long and gray. A lantern hung near his
head, and well beyond him, resting peace-
fully on the farther floor of the cave, were
horses, sheep, and oxen. The man spoke
not save by the beckon of his hand. Without a word they followed him. The
light of the lantern seemed now to glow
with exceeding brightness. They stopped. On the straw before them lay a beautiful young maiden, a child upon her breast.
Her arms, which encircled the babe, her
hands, her head, her whole body, and the
soul within had a glow of fondness. Nature

271

had clothed her for its great event with a fulness of beauty wonderful and yet familiar. In her soft, blue eyes they saw that peace and love which are a part of the ancient, common miracle of God. They saw more, even the light of the world, but were not able to understand. Calmly she looked up at them. Waving strands and masses of golden hair lay above her shoulders and about the head of the child upon her bosom. It was lustrous, beautiful hair, and seemed to glow as the bearded man came near with the lantern. What was there in the tender, peaceful look of the mother, what in her full breasts, what in the breathing of the child, what in the stir of those baby hands to make the soldier bare and bow his head? He leaned against the rock wall of the cave and covered his eyes and thought of his beloved Arria, of his dream of home and peace and little children. The sword fell from his hand. A great sickness of the soul came on him as he thought of those evil days in Jerusalem and

272

of his part in their bloody record. There and then he flung off the fetters of king and emperor.

He knew not yet who lay before him.

As he looked through tears upon them they seemed to be covered with light as with a garment. David knelt before the mother and child in adoration.

Vergilius, full of astonishment, turned to look around him, and saw Manius, who stood near, trembling with superstitious awe. The wonders of the night, the great star and song in the heavens, the glowing cave, the mysterious child and mother had wrought upon him. Were they omens of death?

"Apollo save me!" he whispered, turning to go.

David rose and approached Manius, and spoke with lifted hand.

"Apollo cannot save you," said he. "Kneel! kneel before the sacred mother and put all evil out of your hearts!"

Vergilius knelt, and then his enemy. Manius began to weep.

273

"O God! who hast softened the heart of the world, give us peace!" said David.

Again they heard that voice which had greeted their ears in Jerusalem. It spoke now at the entrance of the cave, saying again: "Where is he that is born king of the Jews?"

David, going to the door of the cave, answered: "Here, within."

"'Tis he — the new king!" the tribune whispered. "I thought kings were born in palaces, and here are they so near the beasts of the field."

Soon came David, and behind him, following in single file, three men, a God-sent majesty in step and countenance. Vergilius and Manius moved aside, saluting solemnly as the men passed. The young tribune turned to his friend and to Manius.

"Come," he whispered. "The Judge of all the earth is here, and, as for me, I dare not remain."

Softly, silently, they departed, their hearts lifted to that peace none may under-

274

stand. Gently, gently, Vergilius took the hand of him who had been his enemy. They had forgotten their bitterness and the touch of awe had made them kin.

"All debts are paid, my brother," said Vergilius. "I forgive you."

He struck his sword deep in the earth. "Henceforth it shall be for a ploughshare," he added.

The assessor bowed low, kissing the hand of Vergilius, who quickly mounted horse.

Then said the latter, turning to his followers: "Come, let us make haste. Before the gold is shining in the great lantern of Shushan I must be on my way to the sea."

"On your way to the sea!" said his friend.

As he answered, the voice of Vergilius had a note of longing and beloved memories: "Yes, for the day is come when I return to the city of Cæsar. Nothing shall separate me longer from my beloved. But come, let us seek Appius at the beacon-fire."

On all sides the great shadow was now thick-sown with stars. The group of horsemen, with colors flying, rode swiftly down the broad way to Jerusalem. Suddenly they drew rein. Great surges of song were rolling in upon this rounded isle from off the immeasurable, mighty deep of the heavens. Beating of drums, and waving of banners, and trumpet-sounds, and battle-cries of them unborn were in that new song —so it seemed to those who heard it. Winding over the gloomy hills near them under the light of the great star, they could see a long procession of shepherds bearing crooks. Awhile the horsemen looked and listened. The host of the dead now seemed to cry unto the host of the living:

"Glory to God in the highest and on earth peace, good-will towards men."

Slowly the song diminished.

"The everlasting gates are lifted up," said David, thoughtfully. Then, thinking of the perils of the new king, he added: "I beseech you, say nothing of these things abroad."

The song had ceased. A cloud, with all its borders bright, now curtained the great star. Another band of horsemen were descending the hill from Bethlehem. Swiftly they came near and halted.

"God send you peace," said the voice of a maiden. "We seek one Vergilius, officer of the cohort."

"And who is he that you should seek him?" said the young tribune, dismounting quickly.

"My lover," said she, a note of trouble in her voice, "and I do fear his life is in peril."

Vergilius was at her side. Now the light of the great star shone full upon them.

"Blood of my heart!" he whispered, lifting the maiden from her horse.

"Oh, you that have made me love you with the great love!" she cried, pressing her cheek upon his. "I have been as one lost in the desert, and I thank the one God he has led me to you."

A moment they stood together and all were silent.

"God has answered my prayer," said he. "But how came you here?"

Then she whispered: "I came with Appius, and the emperor has written that we are to bring you home."

"And we shall live no more apart," said he. "'Tis a night of ten thousand years, dear love. The Christ is come."

"The Christ is come!" she repeated. "How know you?"

"Have you not seen his light in the heavens nor heard the mighty song?"

"Yes, and all the night we have been full of wonder. Listen!"

Again the air trembled with that peal of song:

"Glory to God in the highest, and on earth peace, good-will towards men."

Slowly it sank into silence. Vergilius drew the maiden close and touched her ear with his lips and whispered: "Love has opened our hearts to the knowledge of mighty things. It has led us to the Prince of Peace."

Then said the maiden: "Let us build a temple wherein to worship him, and make it a holy place."

"And call it home," said the young knight, as he kissed her.

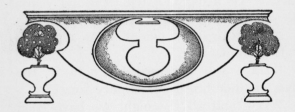

THE END